D.M.T. Journeys

By
Dutch Dimanche

trimarkpress

TABLE OF CONTENTS

1   IN THE BEGINNING

*D*arkness passed through the room, over a book-bag, shirt, and shoes, approaching a bed. The sheets began to rustle, feet moved side to side. Lying on his back, the boy's expression changed. His eyes opened, his head faced the side. There was only darkness. He blinked and something blurry floated near him.

He blinked multiple times as the numbers became vivid on the clock. Three thirty-three in the morning. His eyes started to itch and he attempted to raise his arm to rub them. Nothing happened. He felt heavy, his throat started to itch. The boy thought to himself, *Why can't I feel my arms?*

What once appeared to be a pitch dark room suddenly cleared. He intently looked around. The clock on top of the dresser to the right side of the bed came into focus.

The boy grunted and whimpered and tried to move his fingers, his hand, or even his arms. It felt almost like they were gone completely. He looked down and was relieved to see them. Yet, the heavy feeling grew worse. Both arms, each finger, felt shackled and grew numb. Crushing pain started to overcome him as he tried to move his legs.

His whole body seemed paralyzed. The bed squeaked, giving him a chill feel that something climbed on and slowly crept up to him. The numb feeling worsened from legs to the stomach, as if he were wrapped tightly to the bed. It felt like a two-hundred-pound person sitting on top of him.

He slowly moved his head, painfully feeling every inch of movement. Breathing heavily, he looked down to see his sheets covering him.

Wondering to himself what could be making him feel like this, he spotted a slight shadow movement lowering onto his body. *Bump-bump!* His heart beat faster with the chill of a presence near him, which darkened into the shape of a person.

He glanced at the ceiling, and to his relief, only saw darkness. Suddenly, yellow-glowing eyes shaped like a cat's stared back at him with a hostile glare before turning dark red. The specter was so horrifying it sent a shockwave along his spine. He broke out in a cold sweat and suddenly didn't see anything. A feeling like cold hands wrapped around his throat and he could feel the pressure. He gasped for air and tried to scream for help, but only "H-E-L" came out. His mouth felt dry as if he walked the desert for days without water.

A sinister smile slowly appeared, revealing fangs.

He felt petrified while lying there, slowly ceasing to struggle. He closed his eyes. It felt as though his soul was leaving his body. The creature's eyes turned toward a light that appeared under the door. The faint illumination allowed the boy to see two horns that stuck out of the head.

The hands around his neck lifted and the boy gasped for air as his soul came back to his body. A shadowy head turned back to the boy with an evil glare and the dark figure resumed choking the boy. The light grew brighter, and the door creaked open, and then immediately shut.

The creature vanished. The boy sat straight up and placed his hand on his throat as he looked around the dark room as the numbers on the clock flashed.

Was that real or a nightmare?

He finally fell asleep but then a light shined from under the door. He got up and touched his face and body. *Is that the same light from last night?* Luckily, it was just the sun, which reminded him to get ready for school. He quickly turned to look at the clock as it flashed six thirty-three. He walked into the ensuite bathroom, feeling the cold of the plain white tile floor, and past the small mirror hanging over the sink. He opened the clear curtains, which he picked because he had seen horror movies and knew what could happen when in the shower. He did not want anyone sneaking upon him. Stepping into the cold tub, he turned on the shower and looked up as the water fell onto his face.

He could not stop thinking about what happened. *I don't want to believe it was real, but I have an ominous feeling it was.* Once out of the shower, he toweled off rapidly and headed to his closet. He quickly dressed in his usual blue jeans and grabbed a simple white T-shirt.

Afraid of missing the bus, he hurried toward the door. While twisting the metal doorknob, he thought back to the previous night and wondered what that light was and who opened the door. Directly across from his room was the kitchen with the refrigerator nestled behind a wall, so he knew the light wasn't coming from the refrigerator. To the left of his door were the stairs leading to his grandma's room. But, it couldn't have been his grandma.

She wouldn't open the door then immediately close it. Grandma does not play. She would scream "Boy, wake your but up now!" Plus, those stairs are always squeaking, so you can't sneak up on anyone. She sometimes works the night shift. Is she even home? Oh man, I'm going to miss the bus!

All these thoughts ran through his mind as he grabbed his backpack and darted out of the house and across the front lawn.

He passed the driveway, where his grandma's old green car was usually parked. *I guess she's still working her shift.* Approaching the bus stop, which was down the block, he noticed none of his friends around, which meant he was either early or late for the bus. *Knowing my luck, I'm more than likely late.*

With the day off to such a bad start, he imagined it would only get worse. *Sometimes, I wonder if God has a list of people he doesn't like; if so, I think I'm at the top of it.* While catching his breath and trying to figure out whether he was late, he looked through blurry eyes to see a few people walking toward him.

Hmm, I think that's them... If only this damn sun wasn't in my eyes. He moved up for a clearer view of the shade and bumped into the lamppost. He noticed the peeling paint and wondered about the strange light again. *Maybe it was the lamppost outside my bedroom window that made the light? No, that's dumb — it's outside. Maybe the ceiling light from the kitchen? No, those are way too dim, and I know Grandma didn't change them because she's always too busy.*

DMT JOURNEYS

"Dametrix? Hello? Maybe he's thinking about how stupid and basic he looks wearing those old blue jeans and a white shirt."

He snapped out of the daydream and saw Martino and Stanly approaching.

"It all just screams plain, boring loser," Stanly said with a smug look on his face. Dametrix sized up his outfit, noticing his faded black shirt with "Look at your own business" written on it, pants with some rips, and completely worn out white sneakers.

"Speaking of losers, how's your dad doing!" he shot back with a smirk. "The only thing screaming are those used-to-be white shoes. Half of the jumping man logo on them is completely gone. It looks like he's hopping on one leg to get away from you!"

Martino laughed and shouted, "Oh!"

Then a loud, deep voice yelled out from the distance. "Leave him alone, guys! I like it; it matches his style." Sam approached, wearing his usual basic, yet expensive clothes – a black or white V-neck shirt (today it was black) and his infamous diamond-encrusted cross on a gold chain. He was always sticking up for someone, and talking about how he was going to bring back sexy for dark-skinned people, but that's what happens when you're a six-foottall, seventeen-year-old and everything always seems to go right for you. He had the perfect life with perfect parents that bought him whatever he wanted.

Martino, the youngest of the group, the one Sam called "light bright" or "milk coffee," always adhered to practically everything Stanly, the self-proclaimed boss of the group, said and did. Since both his parents were gone, he had no one except his friends. And his hot, adopted mom. Martino was an adorable kid with curly hair, which Stanly could see too, and he used it to his advantage. Poor kid was always getting into trouble because of Stanly. Both only children, they ended up spending most of their time together, more time than Martino would want.

"Are you OK? Dametrix? Hello?" Dametrix was deep in thought, snapped back to reality, and focused on them.

"Sorry guys, I was thinking about something."

Martino stared at Dametrix innocently with his huge, hazel eyes, waiting to hear what he was going to say next. Stanly, looking at him with impatience, remarked, "What are you waiting for Dumb-cember? For Santa to bring you a gift. By the looks of it, the gift is that dumb look on your face!"

"Nope just your mom," Dametrix shot back, responding to "What are you waiting for?" Martino laughed and through teary eyes continued taunting Stanly. *Yeah, I think Martino doesn't like him that much.*

Dametrix let out a sigh and said, "OK, fine. I'll tell you. Last night, I had a nightmare – well, I think it was a nightmare – that I was in my bed and couldn't move while I was being choked by some creature thing with scary, glowing red eyes. It all felt so real."

They stared at him with blank expressions, except Stanly who, of course, had to comment, "I had the same dream."

He looked at him in surprise and then Martino, with a scared look on his face, said, "Maybe it's the Boogeyman, and he's coming for you guys." Sam, the brave one of the group, looked at Dametrix as if he wanted to say something, but instead, he just laughed nervously and said, "Sorry, Dametrix. I couldn't help it."

Turning to Martino, who still had a scared look, Sam added, "Why are you looking at me as if I just told you that
Santa isn't real?"

"Wait, Santa isn't real?"

"Oh come on, Martino! Are you serious? Aren't you like a fourteen-year-old genius?"

"I'm just playing! I know that. Plus, all my calculations prove it's illogical," Martino replied through laughter. "It's claimed to be magic, but it's still completely impossible. The TV concept of magic isn't real; it's just unexplained science. And Stanly told me

Santa doesn't deliver gifts to people in the hood. If he did, Stanly would see him and pop a cap in his…"

"OK, that's enough," Sam said, interrupting Martino. "Thank you."

"No, let him finish!" Stanly yelled out, unable to keep from laughing. Then he looked at Martino and said, "Yeah, maybe that's what Dametrix saw last night!" Everyone gave him a blank stare. Stanly continued, "How do you know Santa Claus isn't some cover-up by the government to hide the real boogeyman? Or Satan? Claws come on! You know the government has their old pagan traditions…" Martino took a step back.

"Oh no… not this again!" they all uttered, almost in unison.

"…because he's just looking for little boys. Think about it – a magical man all dressed in red comes into your house while everyone else is asleep and leaves you presents.
Where in America is anything really free?"

"You better watch your back, Dametrix. You too Martino. Either one of you could be next," remarked Stanly. "Except you, Sam. You would probably scare him away with all your damn muscles. Are you really even seventeen?"

Later that day in school Dametrix couldn't focus on anything else but what happened to him the night before.

It was like a horror movie playing over and over in his head, and he couldn't escape his thoughts.

On the bus heading home, he heard a faint hiss in his ears, and a chill ran down his spine. Looking around, he realized the bus was quiet. *Maybe I fell asleep on the bus. Please, somebody, wake me up if I did.*

A mysterious voice said, "I'm back to finish what I started…"

He sat, frozen with fear, and stared straight ahead thinking, *No, I'm not going to just let this happen and do nothing like I did last night.* He jumped out of his seat and let out a yelp, startled by the laughter of everyone on the bus. Stanly was doubled over in laughter in the seat behind him. Fed up, he raised a fist toward Stanly.

"Whoa! I'm just kidding. Calm down, pussycat," exclaimed Stanly. "I wanted to tell you something all day, but you seemed so zoned out. I lied… I didn't have that dream like you did. But I noticed it bothering you, so I thought to myself, why don't you just research it online? The way you described your dream to us this morning, it sounded like sleep paralysis. Many people can experience it."

He nodded, thinking he was going to go on one of his conspiracy theory rants about demons or something. For a split second, Dametrix considered interrupting him, but to his surprise, Stanly offered some good advice.

"Wow, here I was thinking you were going to be a jerk about the whole thing. I was ready to cut you off, but you actually have a good idea."

"Yeah, I know. We can stop by the store if you want," Stanly said with a huge smile on his face.

"Why? What do you have to get from the store?"

"A night light! So you don't have to be scared anymore!"

Narrowing his eyes, Dametrix scoffed. "I have a better idea. Let's hang a picture of your face in my room since it scares everyone out of your life!"

His laughter subsided when he finally got the joke. "Hey, that's not funny, Dametrix! Is my face really scary? Wait, where are Martino and Sam?"

"Martino stayed after school because Sam asked him to most likely to try to hang out with that hot girl, Derica. Sam probably had a plan up his sleeve, in this case down his pants. Get it?" Dametrix gave him a look and went back to the seat in front of him. Stanly, still chuckling at his own joke, sat next to him. "He's most likely using our adorable Martino as a wingman to get her. Shame on people these days."

"Don't you do the same thing to get out of trouble with cops?" Dametrix replied accusingly.

"I don't know what you're talking about, besides, that's different. That's a life or death situation."

"Yeah, that you put yourself and him in."

"It's not my fault! People just won't leave me alone even if I'm minding my own business.

"Weren't you recently arrested for trying to rob someone?" Dametrix said.

"Hey, hey, hey. Hold on. That's alleged," Stanly snickered.

"Yeah, right! The only reason they dropped the case is that they felt bad for Martino, who you tried to blame for the whole thing. As always, lucky for you they had no evidence."

"See, that's what I said. People just won't leave me alone."

"You were sprinting away from the house with their front door open and the alarm going off. The cops even called out to you, and you tried to keep running."

"Those pigs only caught me because Martino tripped me, and that's why it was his fault we got caught," Stanly said.

"No, they caught you because you were contemptuous and disrespectful towards them with your arrogance to anything. Martino said the only reason he tripped you was because you tried to do it to him first. Do I even need to take a wild guess why?"

"I don't know what you're talking about," Stanly said and cackled. "Besides, it doesn't matter if you can't prove it. It's invalid – just an unknown that you think you know but can't prove. It's inconclusive. There's your word of the day. Inconclusive."

"You watch too many movies," he replied, shaking his head.

"I can't help it! It's Mom and Dad. Growing up I've learned It's not what you know, it's what you can prove that matters," Stanly remarked. "Hold on. You didn't answer my first question about my face..."

Quickly, to avoid answering the question, Dametrix grabbed his backpack and headed towards the front of the bus. "Look at that; it's my stop. Besides, it's like you said. Inconclusive. You're right. That is a good word. Bye Stan. Oh, and thanks for the tip!"

Walking towards his two-story blue house, he glanced at the driveway, hoping to see his grandma's car, but it wasn't there. *I guess she picked up another night shift.* He unlocked the front door and headed inside. The house always seemed empty. He should be used to this by now, and it shouldn't have bothered him. She worked hard for them both. But, just once, it would be nice to have her home for more than a day. *All I want is to have some family time with my grandma and have a nice home-cooked meal instead of a frozen dinner or leftovers.*

If she were here, she would know what to do about the creature from last night. She always had the answers. His grandma was so smart and told the funniest jokes.

She was the only family he had. Dametrix didn't know much about his parents or the rest of the family. Whenever he asked about them, his grandma seemed to always change the subject or say she doesn't want to talk about it – "It's time for bed, we'll talk another time." He wondered if something tragic happened. Or maybe they were super spies for the government and had to give up their lives to protect the country. *Although with my luck, they probably stepped outside, and a meteor fell on them.*

Walking into his bedroom, he realized how dark the room and everything in it was – all black furniture, including his black laptop sitting on the corner of the black bed with black and white pillows and sheets. *Out of all the colors, why did I pick black for everything?* He quickly turned on all the lights, dropped his backpack, sat down on the bed to take off his shoes and the bed squeaked, jump-starting the memory of last night. Making him more determined. He turned on the laptop. Thinking about what Stanly told him, he searched the Internet for sleep paralysis.

Thousands of different websites popped up. Most of the websites just explained scientists' definitions:

"During episodes of sleep paralysis, the sufferer awakens to rapid eye movement sleep-based atonia combined with conscious awareness. This is usually a frightening event often accompanied by vivid, waking dreams (i.e., hallucinations)."

Unfortunately, these websites were useless to him. Yeah, yeah, yeah. *Scientists always think they know it all. Oh man, I sound like Stanly.*

Last night felt too real for it to be his dreams or some hallucination. He scrolled until he found a website that caught his attention. "Oh, this looks interesting..." he said aloud.

"Dating back to the olden days, some people believe this supernatural phenomenon to be demons." Along with the article were pictures, drawings, and paintings of what people in the old days believed was the cause of the strange occurrence. One picture showed what appeared to be a creature sitting on someone. This picture had several comments from people, and some of the comments were posted recently. One girl, Jessica, wrote: *"My little brother keeps experiencing this. Does anyone know how I can help him?"* A ton of other people shared their stories; some were more severe than others.

Whoa, this one seems eerily similar to mine. He stared at the screen, continuing to read story after story explaining aliens, spiders, and people who resembled snakes, and had a sensation of the creature's creepy smile directed at him.

Glancing around the room, he noticed dark areas as though something was hiding within, just waiting for the perfect moment to sneak upon him. The closet was across from his bed, and even though the door was open, only pitch black was visible. Suddenly, his room felt small, like the walls were closing in on him.

Grabbing his laptop, he bolted to the bathroom, and turned on all the lights. Now, it felt like he was sitting next to the sun. Suddenly, a website ad popped up offering ways to stop sleep paralysis.

This is probably a bunch of nonsense. Can you even cure it? He clicked the link.

"Sleep paralysis most commonly occurs right after you fall asleep or wake up. Once in a dream-like state, you are aware of your surroundings but unable to move any or all of your muscles known as atonia. Sleep paralysis can be the gateway to lucid dreaming. During a lucid dream, you're aware you're dreaming and can learn to gain control of your dream characters and environment."

The article went on to explain how you can even train your brain to have lucid dreams.

"Keep track of your dreams in a journal and review it regularly to look for any patterns. It also helps you realize when you are in a dream. If you are in a dream remember to perform reality checks, like observing your hands which tend to be distorted in dreams. This can help you confirm whether you're awake or asleep."

He felt uncomfortable, so he clicked off the page and continued searching through the thousands of website results. More than half of the results were of people sharing more of their stories of sleep paralysis with similar photographs of what they encountered, including demons that loomed over them. Evil spirits chasing after them.

He had an uneasy feeling that the room wasn't bright enough, despite that every light in the room and bathroom was turned on. Damn, Stanly has me so paranoid.

After spending hours online and reading dozens of articles, his eyes were red and irritated from being rubbed constantly. He was fighting off the sleep he so desperately needed. His back was sore, his legs were numb, and he couldn't even feel his feet anymore. He closed his laptop and thought about everything he just read. It seems lucid dreaming is the best way to help against sleep paralysis. *Well, that or the website's talking about doing yoga, getting proper sleep exercising. That sounds boring. I can see it now, Stanly making fun of me. There's no way I'm doing yoga. First thing's first, I need to track all my dreams in a journal. Then I can start to recognize when I'm in a dream and can try to change it.*

A big smile spread across his tired face.

It seemed he was asleep for only a short while before he opened his eyes, and it was morning. The sun shined brightly through the window. *Oh no, the bus! Not again!* Just like the day before, he quickly threw on some clothes, grabbed his backpack, and raced outside to the bus. As he neared the bus stop, he saw the bus pulling away, so he chased after it. Hoping for the bus driver to see him or stop at a red light, he continued to chase the bus for a few blocks. He grew suspicious that every time he was about to catch up, the bus driver drove faster. Eventually, he stopped to pick up the next group of kids and was able to get on. *After all the times I've been late and had to chase after the bus, you would think I would be faster and able to catch it.*

Once he got on the bus, everyone laughed at him. Except for Derica. Even though they had only spoken a handful of times, she was the only girl that he felt comfortable around, besides his grandma. Plus, the few times she said "Hi" to him were awesome. He headed toward the back of the bus to find a seat. A short while after he sat down, the bus driver pulled into the school parking lot and opened the doors to let them all off. He yelled breathlessly, "Oh come on, really?"

Like the day before, the school day flew by. The next few weeks went by in a blur. The only thing he could focus on was lucid dreaming and how to master it. All he wanted to do was sleep and practice lucid dreaming.

He wrote every dream he could remember in his journal. *According to some research found on dreams, people always have dreams but may not remember them. Remember the words of Laberge: Always be alert. It is said that making yourself aware that you are in a dream will help you to remember the dream.* This piece of advice was a huge help for him in learning how to control his dreams.

In one of my reoccurring dreams, I am trying to save Derica from an evil shark-man hybrid that tried to kidnap her. At first, I didn't think I could control anything in the dream despite how real it felt. The dream felt so real and scary that I woke up in a cold sweat. After realizing I was safely in my room, I forced myself back to sleep, to have the same dream, and surprisingly, continued the same dream.

Martino stared at him as he told the stories on the bus.

He went home and had the same recurring dream where the evil shark-man kidnapped Derica. After a short battle, he saved her, and taunted the shark-man with the nickname *Bubbles*, which infuriated him more.

In another dream, Dametrix was on a pirate ship sailing with both Blackbeard and Black Caesar, and can you guess who was in the water circling the ship? It was Bubbles. Once Dametrix saw him, he immediately started mocking him by calling him Bubbles again. He liked the pirate dream, so he tried to dream about it more. He watched pirate movies and went to bed thinking about pirates. Once asleep, the dream always started the same way. He was on the boat, and the crew shouted, "Ye, first mate, Dametrix, is here!" Then somehow, every time Bubbles appeared on deck in front of him. His body was fit and covered in smooth grey scales with little fins on each of his calves and forearms. He was wearing his usual ripped pants that looked like he'd been wearing them since he was a kid. With each dream, his face resembled a human face more and more. One time, Dametrix was able to see it clearer, and it looked eerily similar to his own face.

"OK, Bubbles. It's been fun, but I have to get rid of you and your tight pants once and for all. Don't get me wrong. I love sharks, but you give them a bad name," he said. The shark-man usually grunted or growled back at him, so he never heard him actually speak, but Dametrix could tell the constant name-calling finally got to him this time.

The shark-man let out a few grunts before replying, "Stop calling me Bubbles. I hate that damn name. My name is Gala." His voice sounded like there was water constantly stuck in his throat.

"I don't care what your name is," Dametrix said. "I don't know how or why, but you keep ending up in my dreams." Dametrix punched him and that sent him flying across the ship, causing the ship to rock back and forth and water to splash up over the sides.

What was once a sunny day now suddenly shifted to pouring rain. Gala stood up and wiped the blood from his mouth, giving Dametrix one of the angriest expressions he had ever seen.

A deafening roar filled the air. At first, he thought it was Gala, but, he peered over the side of the ship and saw a huge squid-like sea creature.

"It's the Kraken," cried out a cowardly crew member. Bubbles smiled. Dametrix turned back to him and shouted, "Why are you smiling? Is that your girlfriend coming to save you?" His smile immediately turned to a frown as he angrily ran towards Dametrix. He threw a punch, but Dametrix jumped before it reached him. Gala grabbed his legs and pulled him down to the ground. He stood to see a fist heading straight for his face. Bubbles was able to land his punch this time and sent his head spinning.

He wiped the blood off his lip and smiled back at Bubbles. "I'm sorry Bubbles. That was probably your mom!" Dametrix grabbed him by the throat and leaped into the air and the two-headed toward the sea of the violent waves. Attempting to seize Dametrix with a tentacle, the Kraken stared at him with its massive, black eyes and let out a thunderous roar. Bubbles' once angry expression was now one of fear. He clutched Dametrix's arm and yelled. A faint smile spread across his face as he let go of Bubbles.

"Bye-bye, Bubbles."

Falling towards the Kraken's open mouth, Bubbles cried out, "I'll be back!"

"Dead man tells no tales," Dametrix said and laughed.

Since he had been having this same dream for weeks, he decided to tell Stanly, Martino, and Sam about it on the bus ride home one day. They all just stared at him, wideeyed.

Martino finally spoke. "That sounds like an awesome dream."

"Yeah, it's much better than the one you told us about the boogeyman that tried to molest you," remarked Stanly.

"And that's the last you'll hear of my dreams, you bum," Dametrix quipped back to Stanly.

The bus arrived at his stop, so he grabbed his things and hurried off, eager to get back to sleep and dream. "Bye everyone, except Stanly!" And he jumped off the bus.

"Why are you always running off? Why don't you ever hang out with us anymore?" Stanly said as he stuck his head out the bus window.

"Because I still never found that night light for the Boogeyman!"

 "Aww, come on, man! That was a joke from weeks ago! I'll listen to all your dreams and not say anything."

"Bye, Stanly! See you later, buddy!" All Dametrix could think about was taking some time out from seeing his friends and putting in more sleeping time. Finally, he reached his room and collapsed onto his bed to start his wonderful dream adventures.

2 THINK BEFORE YOU DO

*O*nly darkness filled the room as Dametrix blinked his eyes open. The terrifying feeling of all this happening before washed over him. Quickly sitting up in bed, his eyes scanned the room, from ceiling to closet. *Am I awake or asleep?*

Suddenly, he heard a tapping noise coming from the window. He hopped out of bed and ran out of the room.

Even though leaving the room made him feel a little better, he kept running in the dark until he hit something hard.

He tried to slowly feel around to better understand what it was. Because he didn't remember leaving anything outside his door. *It's the handle to the upper part of the stairs. How could this be unless I was in my grandma's room?*

The whole house was pitch black, but he slowly crept back to look in the room to see if it was her room. He saw the outline of what appeared to be his grandma's bed, against the blue-ish light coming from the window. The bed was still made. *Why isn't she home yet?*

He stood at her doorway and stared down the steps. He left the door open, the blue light coming from the window bright enough. Only the first step was visible, and the rest disappeared into the darkness. Looking around, he tried to discern the shapes of shadows. They appeared to be getting closer, and he heard the tapping sound again. Only this time, it was louder. With the darkness consuming everything around him, he bolted downstairs. His first step made a loud creak. He thought if he rushed, the noise wouldn't be as bad, but instead, it was the opposite − every step creaked loudly. It felt like something, or someone, was following him. *Why do these things happen at the worst times?*

DMT JOURNEYS

Downstairs, it felt colder than usual. He headed toward the front door and looked around into the darkness, trying to find the doorknob. This time, shadows and movement caught his attention in the darkness. He froze and blinked multiple times. *Are my eyes playing tricks on me or is something actually there?*

He extended his hand to the doorknob. A loud *BANG!* echoed throughout the house. His heart raced. He froze. He heard another loud *BANG!* He panicked, unsure of where the noise was coming from, and struggled with the door before finally opening it. Standing in the doorway was a young white man, maybe in his early twenties, with long black hair and piercing blue eyes. He wore a white shirt covered in paint stains and ripped blue jeans. "Whoa, dude. What's the rush?" he said, surprisingly calm.

Dametrix was speechless. *This can't be real.*

"Can you speak? My name is David," he said, focusing all his attention on him.

Dametrix tried to open his mouth to speak, but nothing came out.

"Calm down, man" he exclaimed. Then he smacked Dametrix's face. "Just breathe and relax. Think of the word you want to say and focus on saying it." Dametrix let out a loud "ow." The mysterious man laughed and said, "You're a funny little guy."

Finally, catching his breath and rubbing his cheek, Dametrix said, "Who are you? And why did you slap me?"

"Hmm, how can I explain this? You know when a baby is born and the doctor slaps them to get a reaction? Well, congrats, you were just born into the dream state ."

"What are you doing at my house?" he asked, not fully understanding what he was just told.

"Technically, little dude, this isn't your house anymore. What I mean is this is actually your dream world house.
I can see the confused look you're giving me and bet you have dozens of questions. So, aren't you going to invite me inside to chat?"

"Oh, sorry, where are my manners? Come in, David." His reply sounded overly proper. As his grandma always said, *"Without manners, we're no different from animals."* Those rules are what keeps us from turning into one.

"Great! I'll show you how it works. See, in the dream world kitchen, you can think of almost anything, and if you're good enough, it will appear. In your kitchen, think of any food you want and it'll appear. You've done this more than enough times, it should be a piece of cake. Get it? Ha ha. OK, moving on. Imagine now, you go to the kitchen where you commonly go to get food and think of something you would normally grab to eat. I'll stand by the stairs. It can get a little messy for first-timers. OK, go." Dametrix looked at him, confused.

"Hello, little dude," David said. "Why are you looking at me like that? Are you OK?"

Standing in the kitchen, facing David, the only thing he could do was lift his hand and point to the hallway behind David. Slowly turning around, David finally saw what Dametrix saw, a giant figure with glowing red eyes, covered in a black cloak. Dametrix made a bee-line for the front door. As soon as he moved, the creature jumped over David and flew across the living room after Dametrix, lunged, and tackled him to the ground. Dametrix could feel its icy grip on his legs as it attempted to drag him.

A .50 caliber gun appeared in David's right hand before Dametrix could even open his mouth to scream. David grabbed Dametrix's left hand, then pulled the trigger, causing a dark blue beam to fire and hit the hooded figure, sending it flying across the house.

David scooped him up and leapt into the air to fly away from the house. Once they were a safe distance away, David extended his arm and opened his hand, exposing a swirly black hole in his palm. They were instantly sucked into the hole, where they saw nothing but swirling colors. David gave him a reassuring look and said, "You can relax now. We're in a portal heading to the dream realm where the dream world is. The night ghoul can't follow us there. Plus, it's the coolest place you can ever go to. Only strong dreamers can get here."

"I'm guessing the night ghoul is what grabbed me back there." Words went back and forth in his head. *Should I ask him? Seems like he would be able to help me.* He finally said, "You sure know a good amount about them. Do they all look like the one we just saw? Or are there different types? I think one attacked me outside of my dream. Everyone kept telling me that I was just dreaming, but it felt so real. It didn't look like this one. I'll never forget its evil smile that showed off all its long yellow teeth or the pressure I felt when it pressed down on me."

"I've never heard of night ghouls attacking people outside of their dreams. I only know of two kinds of night ghouls, and neither one sounds like what you described," exclaimed David. "Aha, we're almost there."

Dametrix shifted his focus from David to where they were heading: a stretched out world with bright stand-out features, like these were personally made by someone. The domain had lights on four corners, one to the east, west, and so on. Over the flat earth-circle water fell at the edge covering a desolate and waste part under the earth. David said that the dead-looking area was called the *tohu va-bohu*, and the area under the water falling off the edge was called the *beliy-mah*. In other words, the flat circle of earth laid between the chaotic waters above and the chaotic waters below. That was also the name given to what he was surprised to see. The huge half-sphere looked similar to the earth – mostly green than blue – and a colorful city lay ahead. A a wall at end of the city cut it off from the edge of the world. It came into view the closer they got and he could see there weren't many buildings, just fields of grass and people flying around everywhere. High above the city, floating in the clouds, was a huge castle. Bright knights in shining armor stood above the city and near the castle, each equipped with a sword or spear. As they passed by the knights stationed at the city's gates, David smiled at them, but only received cold, statuesque looks back as they followed them with their eyes.

"That's creepy," David whispered. "I've never seen them do that. I've passed through here multiple times, and I've never gotten those stares before. Definitely not them following me with their eyes. Are you sure you've never been here? Their eyes seemed focused on you."

"Yes, I'm sure I've never been to this world or seen them before. Now, put me down!" Dametrix was a bit agitated because he was still cradled David's arms. "They're probably giving us those stares because we were just attacked by something and look a mess. Speaking of that, you never told me what you were doing at my house."

"Oh right. Sorry, little dude I was lost. It's strange how they were looking at you. It's the same look that night ghoul was giving you at your house like they're scared of you or something…" he replied while finally landing and letting him go. "OK, there are some rules I have to explain before we go any further. Plus, it seems like trouble follows you, and I don't want trouble."

"Those bright knights are called Watchers, and just as the name says, they watch over the dream world and protect it from ghouls or anything evil. Think of them as cops, but the good kind. I don't know much about them, except that they're very powerful and come from the castle up there." David explained, pointing upward toward the huge castle floating above them. It is called the castle firmament. "First thing's first, there are three major rules that everyone must know and obey. Follow them, and you'll be good. Rule one: don't bug the big scary looking watchers. I'm sure that's obvious. There was this guy who once tried to go into the castle by making himself look like them. Trust me, he didn't get far. I guess they saw through his disguise. They're called Watchers."

"Come on, dude, surely they can see better than us and aren't so easily fooled. Now he's stuck in a bubbler." Normally Dametrix liked that word and wouldn't say no, but this time he did.

With a big smile on his face, David went on, "OK, anyhoo, guess you don't get it. A bubbler is half and half. It's like a dream house or your own dream world. It can be a good thing or bad, but you don't want the watchers to put you in one.

"Every time you dream, it's either the same lame dream or you don't dream at all and forget you were ever here. You wonder if this was real or make-believe. I guess that was his punishment. Rule two: don't harm any other person here. You want to fight, we have a battle royale, but after that, that's it. We don't bug the person, try to make this a nightmare for them, or you get the bubbler or bubble. Rule three: this is the most important rule. Don't ever, ever, ever go through the dark door. See this big wall with a dark door on it? See, on the other side of the city suddenly they just disappear and reappear in front of the wall."

As David talked, a voice called Dametrix closer towards the door. As he heard it say loudly, "Come closer, I'm here, come, come," he reached out to touch the doorknob. David slapped his hand away and Dametrix snapped out of the trance. David asked incredulously, "What are you doing man. Come on, man, did you not just hear me dude? Don't touch the big scary-looking door."

"Sorry, how did you do it?"

"Do what?"

"Make that voice call me?"

"Man, I didn't do anything! Are you OK dude? You are hearing voices now. Don't tell me you're going crazy." David glanced at the strange door then looked back. "That door is weird. Come here, man, it's dangerous." They walked away. "A lot of people get curious and think they are strong, and they lose their life being nosy, going in there, never coming out. The only one I've ever seen come out alive is one of the Watchers. And he was pretty beat up. If you go anywhere near that door, you know you're going to get it. Got it?"

"Yeah, the bubble, calm down. I'm not going in there," Dametrix replied, exasperated.

"OK good. Do you have any questions, little dude?"

Still rubbing and looking at his hand, Dametrix fired off his questions. "What created the ghouls? What makes them how they are? Were they always here? Why don't the Watchers just go in the dark door to get rid of them? How come I've never been here before? I lucid dream but never here or what you called my dream house. How do I know this is real and not another dream?"

David interrupted him after giving him a blank stare. "Alright, little dude relax. Those are good questions. I've never asked those questions. You can feel free to ask the scary, big looking, bright guys, if you want. Most people just leave them alone and go about their dreams because they know the watchers will protect and save them. The only reason why I could think of why you have never been here or seen your dream house is that you weren't a strong enough dreamer. There are different levels and types of dreams. You obviously need to have experience to master or experience them. If not, you would end up like everyone else, little dude, in regular dreams where your subconscious creates your dreams for you, a.k.a., your dream bubble. Some get lucky and are able to experience the different types like lucid dreaming. Some people say that they have seen the future or different realms through sleep. You ever have a dream that felt so real? Don't you ever wonder why some call it deja vu? I am sure you've at least experienced scenarios like that little dude. In here people believe that dreams are a powerful thing. Can you blame them if they did not pursue their curiosity? This would never be, and no one would really be here. The list goes on and on man, of the mysteries and wonderful places you can travel through sleep. Of course, where there is good bad follows, man. I believe what happened to you is that your subconscious created the dream for you, either because of a trauma, past experience, or emotions triggering it.

"Maybe you became stronger than you know and broke out of your dream bubble sending yourself into the dream world. Happens to some who reach their happy place, within their dream realm and end up in the dream world. What I do know about ghouls is that most of them

DMT JOURNEYS

were once people. Before you learn how you must know this. Your body has a balance of two important sources of energy, kinda like yin and yang.

"Your outer and eternal energy. Inner energy, get it, in-er-gy." Dametrix stared as David looked at him expectantly, his hands like a jester. He sighed. "OK anyhoo, you use your outer energy kinda like physically doing stuff, like your daily routine – things like going to work, school society, same old boring stuff. When it's all used up it makes you tired. You have to rest or sleep to restore your outer energy.

"While you sleep, you use your inner energy. That's what helps you dream and do cool stuff in your dream. That can get used up so your body wakes you up before it happens. That's why when you have a good dream, you don't want to wake up from it, but still end up doing so. Then you go about your boring life and give your inner energy a chance to restore itself.

"Sometimes you don't listen to that alarm clock and sleep for too long, then wake up tired because you unbalanced yourself. Usually, you go back to normal. Then, there are unfortunate people – those who die in their sleep, end up getting stuck in the dark door, or just can't wake up. People who get stuck in the dream world lose all their inner energy and end up having to feed on others' energy.

"Once they get a taste, they crave it and get addicted, rather than start to depend on it. Next thing you know, you become a nightmare ghoul. If you're feeding on someone for too long, you give them nightmares. Sometimes they purposely give you nightmares 'cause you release more energy being scared and if you do it for too long, the nightmare becomes scarier. That's why you wake up since your in-ergy is draining fast. They can even end up killing the people they feed on or put them in a coma just to keep feeding. People can either get taken away by the watchers to the castle, which I'm guessing is a way to heaven, so they won't do the same thing and become ghouls themselves.

"That's enough talking about the lame stuff. Don't think about it too much, man. Do you want me to show you how to create things like this nice gun? Remember what I said back at the dream house, it's all in your head. If you can think of it, you can create it and try to picture something like a gun or sword. Just focus your mind on how it'll feel and look like."

Dametrix was staring at his hands and focusing hard.

"OK, OK, you can stop. Dude, you look like you have to use the bathroom. Let me show you." Just as he said that multiple guns showed up in his hands. One disappeared and another bigger one appeared soon after.

Dametrix was amazed. "Wow, how are you able to do that?! You seem to know a lot about weapons too."

"Yeah man, believe it or not, I wanted to be in the military, mostly the air force," David replied, his eyes beginning to glaze over. "Flying planes and doing spy missions. I'm guessing you never did it." Dametrix was about to press for more when he was cut off. "Little dude, I don't want to talk about it."

"Why not? Tell me, tell me, tell me, tell me, tell me!"

"OK man, stop asking!" David said with a big smile. "I'm afraid I don't want to grow up. I watch people and my mom struggle. Work hard, grow tired, and not have fun. Then I realized being an adult isn't all that fun. You have to pay a lot of money for bills and stuff you don't want to pay for. It's all so you can live a life most people call normal. You go to a job you don't enjoy just earning money to spend on the stuff you don't really want to. From what my mom always says, you don't get to make enough money to enjoy life. You just make enough money to pay for bills. She said it's the corporate world's way of keeping you chained and controlling you in order for you to obey them."

Dametrix was surprised. "Well, I never thought about it that way. I've grown up without my mom and dad, barely knowing anything about them. My grandma is always working, so maybe what you said is true, but my grandma doesn't seem to have a problem with it, she's always happy. It can't be that bad if you just get the right job and spend money wisely. I'm sure it isn't that horrible. Look at rich people, how do you think they made it? Hard work. Well, not the spoiled kids, the hard-working ones, at least. My friend Sam says his parents work hard, are rich, and they try to make sure he has a good future. He doesn't seem to have a problem with it. I think life is what you make it. Yeah, it's scary but what isn't scary the first time you do it? Just be smart about your decisions and work hard to get what you want."

David smiled and laughed. "That's such a little kid thing to say and also grown up. I think you're right, little dude, I mean, man."

They smiled at each other. David put his hand on Dametrix's shoulder. "You seem trustworthy and you are going to make a great adult. I'm going to teach you something cool, not many people here know how to do it."

A wide smile filled Dametrix's face with excitement. "What is it? Tell me!"

"Have you ever wanted to enter someone else's dream?" David asked.

The first person who came to Dametrix 's mind was Stanly. Thinking about all the ways he would torment him, he let out a menacingly hysterical laugh.

David shushed him. "The Watchers, dude, they can't know I'm teaching you this! We can get in a lot of trouble for this."

DMT JOURNEYS

They walked into a building that looked similar to a bar in Western movies. The people there looked like TV characters. Dametrix's mouth opened, fascinated by the strange sight before him. David looked over at him. "Cool, huh? Don't get too excited, it's not real. They're just people who make themselves look like their favorite characters. It's only once in a blue moon when you see someone that actually looks like who they are. Picture this as one big comic's convention – people living out their fantasy."

Dametrix replied, "Really? I've never been to one, but man this is what they look like. Cool. It's Spawn, my fave, and Goku."

"Come on, let's go, we have to hurry. Time is running out and we are heading to the back where the watchers don't pay much attention to or sense us," David said.

"Oh my gosh, it's Naruto!"

"Let's go, man!" Dametrix ran and yelled "OK!" as he followed David to the back room.

"This room is dark," David said as his voice echoed, "because this is the center of the dream world. It was created by those who were here before me and you, the legends of the beliy-mah. They were able to do anything in their dreams.

"No one really knows what happened to them. Some say they became Watchers. Others said the Watchers took them." A light appeared in David's hand, lighting up the whole room. "OK. In order to enter someone else's dream, you have to show me you can control your own. Now, manifest a chair right now. Just concentrate on remembering a chair and what it would feel like in your hands. Your mind will do the rest."

Dametrix looked at David, doubting himself.

"Come on man, you have to have some imagination left!"

After staring at his hand for a few seconds, a plain, white lawn chair appeared and Dametrix smiled in disbelief. David looked at it and laughed hard.

"What's so funny?"

"You see how plain this chair is? That's how your imagination and attention to detail is. Only plain, but that will do noob. Whose dreams would you like to go into? You have to be sure they are asleep. This is the outside time; you need to be sure they are going to be asleep. If not, we might end up in a random place."

Dametrix snickered and smiled wide, looked at David's hand and said, "Yeah, I know that pain in the butt is sleeping. It's three in the morning. How are you able to tell real time? Can I do it too?"

David grimaced and let out a whimper. "You can try if you want."

"Why the snicker?"

"'Cause your mind is in the dream world, man, you can't bring stuff with you. Some things can astral project into the realm of dreams, but it takes an immensely powerful person to do that."

Dametrix was about to ask about the person when David interrupted him. "Do you want to keep asking questions or do you want to learn how to get into your friend's dream?"

"Enough about ways to get into the dream realm. Try to think of how your friend usually is and what he would most likely be dreaming or where he is. If you could do an astral projection, we would've just been able to reach there."

"Wait, maybe I can astral project," Dametrix said. "I kinda did it once. You told me everything in the dream world is visualizing and remembering. Maybe I can try to remember how it felt and try to do it." David looked at him for a minute and laughed. "Come on man, you just entered the dream world. Now you're expecting to astral project out of it? Let me do it first, man, then you can practice. Since your eyes are closed already because you're asleep, you would have to try to take a deep breath and imagine you were trying to move outside of your body. It takes hard work, and that is just the basic step. Dude, some people can do some things. Not everyone can do everything, even in the dream world."

"If there's one thing I hate in life is when someone tells me I can't do something," Dametrix said. He closed his eyes. "Life is a blank sheet of paper. You make it how it is since the paper is already there. Everyone has their own sheet of paper. Some are more blank while others have the lines and guides. You have the power to draw the picture, write how you want your paper to say or look. Don't write or tell me what to do with my paper."

"Dude, what are you doing?! Oh my gosh, stop!" David grabbed Dametrix to try to stop him. The room lit up and the door swung open. David screamed, surprised at what was staring at him. It was a watcher appearing in a flash of light, with yellow eyes, looking at them with shock and anger. David quickly thrust out his arm and grabbed Dametrix. "Hurry, hurry!" he screamed.

They sank into the ground. Another bright flash came in yellow streaks. It moved towards David to grab what was left of his hand and then they completely disappeared into the ground. Out came Dametrix holding on tight to David. A hand reached out and disappeared. David loosened his grip and tried to hang on to Dametrix's leg. He was curled up like a scared kid who didn't want to fall.

Dametrix opened his eyes. "What are you screaming about?" David didn't answer. A body and a hand came out from what appeared to be Dametrix's head. He shrieked and looked around. What had he done?

"Oh my gosh, man, I can't believe you did it! You're astral projecting!" David said.

Dametrix stared at his hand. He saw so many different colors, rings, and waves. It was like being submerged an in an ocean of wonders and swirling colors. It was like water moving back and forth on a beach.

Both stared at the beautiful sight. Dametrix whispered in awe. "This is the most beautiful thing I've ever seen. If I didn't see it I couldn't even believe it myself."

"I agree man," David replied. "This is something you can't even describe – it's what everyone talks about in stories of people who actually did it. But they never described this feeling. I feel so free, so light, so scared so… at peace."

Dametrix replied, "Yeah dude, I can't believe it myself." Looking at his clear, yet pure, white hands, he saw the details of his hands, yet he could see right through them. They were different colors and it seemed like something was coming off his hands, like a vibration. Like sonar. Every time he moved it created a ring of what looked like sound waves that sounded like a heartbeat. *Bump, bump, bump, bump*. Every bump was a vibrating echo spreading like a sonar wave. He looked at David – his vibration was small, light, and faint. David looked back at him "OK dude, let's focus, hurry, and find your friend before it's too late."

Dametrix looked confused. "What do you mean by that? Why do you look different from me?"

"I don't know man, everyone is different."

"How do I fly, David? I'm worried I'm just floating here."

David replied, "You see how you float up and down like you're in an ocean? Think of a really good moment or feeling of your life. Hold that feeling inside. Feel yourself free-floating flying, which is like swimming if you think about it. The energy around you is the water. Float on it using your mind as the wheel and your emotions as your gas. Your own energy as your fire to give you a push. Moving you in the direction you want to go. Try it, feel and think about where you want to go and just do it."

Dametrix closed his eyes again. "It worked before, so why not again?"

David grabbed him, straining to pull him forward with all his might. Nothing happened. He pulled and tugged, but still nothing happened. "Man, this is harder than in the dream world! Why is it so difficult now? He stood with his hand on his chin, rubbing on his little scruff of beard. While Dametrix slowly floated away on his stomach. David grabbed onto him and they flew away fast. David yelled, "Open your eyes, man, open them!"

Dametrix opened his eyes and they stopped. There they floated, right above Stanly. A smile stretched on Dametrix's face.

"Wow dude, are you sure you haven't done this before?" David asked. "The next thing I'm going to teach you is really dangerous to do. We're going to enter his dream. Once you do, try to connect with everything you see because there's an energy flow present in the dream. Copy it and realize your own energy projecting your imagination onto his world. I'll change the environment and you change into what you want to."

Dametrix, who bounced up and down with excitement, said, "Yeah ,yeah, yeah, let's just do it already. I think I figured out this whole dream thing!"

It was a sunny day. Stanly was happy and smiling while a small nut fell down in front of him. He grabbed it and a dark, brown squirrel with a fluffy tail came by and stared at him. Sitting up and looking at the creature, Stanly smiled. "Hey Mr. Squirrel, is this a nut? Well, you can't have it." Laughing loudly, he looked at the little squirrel who was staring back at him, now with red eyes, almost appearing as if it was smiling back at him. "I'm just playing, Mr. Squirrel, you can have it back."

He threw it in front of the squirrel. It looked at him with dark red eyes and a smile with the front teeth showing. With a deep voice, the squirrel said, "No, you're the one that's nuts and I want you."

Stanly gave the squirrel a confused look. Replying to what he thought he heard, he asked, "Did you say something, Mr. Squirrel?"

The sky changed quickly, with dark clouds gathering and lightning bolts. The squirrel's eyes started to get darker with maroon-red pupils. The squirrel grew larger until it was eight feet tall. "You heard me boy, come here, I'm going to eat you!" Stanly fell and quickly got up and ran away, yelling "I'm sorry Mr. Squirrel, it was a joke!"

The squirrel chased and grabbed Stanly, staring at him with a devilish, sinister stare. "Your time has come to pay for all that you have done, little boy." Stanly screamed and cried while trying to get free. "I'm sorry, please Mr. Squirrel, I'm sorry. Please don't eat me, I've been a good boy."

The squirrel roared in his face, saliva flying everywhere and splashing on Stanly's face as he stared at the deep darkness inside the squirrel's mouth. "OK, maybe I've not been that good but who has, right? I'm only human; plus it's everyone else's fault." The squirrel angrily stared at him. When it was about to open its mouth, Stanly quickly yelled. "OK wait, what do you want me to do? Fine I lied, but you can't prove it. What do you want from me?"

DMT JOURNEYS

The squirrel with its deep voice replied, "When you see your friend Dametrix, apologize and tell him you wet the bed."

Stanly looked at the squirrel very confused, yet scared. "OK fine, I'll do it, just don't kill me. I don't want to die." The alarm rang.

Stanly's eyes opened. He quickly sat up in his bed, thinking, "Wait, was that real or a dream?" He thought more and laughed out loud. "Oh well, it was really funny."

Running to the bus stop, Dametrix thought, "Ugh, I hope I'm not late again." When he got there, everyone at the bus stop was talking except for Stanly. Dametrix said hello as Stanly awkwardly looked at him. Martino and Sam stared at Stanly, then Dametrix, waiting to see if he would say something. Instead Stanly stayed oddly quiet, thinking of whether the vision with Mr. Squirrel really happened. The bus pulled up and they heard the tires roll on the ground, making a crumbling noise, and the brakes squealed as the bus stopped.

The moment the doors opened, Stanly could hear other kids chatting as he sat down next to Dametrix. It was a quiet bus ride for Stanly as he tried to play it cool by talking a little. The guys told Dametrix to ask why he was acting odd, who was thinking, "I have a strong feeling I did invade his dream. Oh my gosh, that's so cool!" *Wait, why hasn't he said what I told him to say?*

They arrived at school and there was Westly Deon, or as Dametrix called him, W.D., at the lockers picking on a kid as usual; this time it was Bartimaeus, who was just trying to get his stuff. W.D. slapped him behind his head then slammed him against the lockers repeatedly, taking his glasses off. His eyesight was so bad, he was practically blind without the glasses.

"Come on, give me your money, you little punk." Dametrix thought it was a part of life. When you're tall and pale you can pick on those smaller than you who can't defend themselves. That wasn't even the sad part. What made it worse is that everyone ignored it, not saying or doing anything about it.

Luckily for those in the group, W.D. didn't bug them because of Sam. Dametrix wouldn't want to fight Sam either. He tried to bully Stanly once, but he was no pushover and didn't care how big you were or who you were. He also almost stabbed W.D once when they almost fought. *Ha ha, man that was funny until we found out the reason was because Stanly was trying to rob him. You would think for a kid that's always doing something bad he would always get caught. I wonder if he does it on purpose or just leaves some kind of clue so you know it's him. Cause just doing something bad isn't a thrill anymore, the next level is leaving a mark, hoping you almost get caught. That thrill of the hunt adrenaline rush.*

W.D., the five-foot eleven-inch bully, held back. He was a chunky sports player with pale skin. *Isn't that mostly the case with most bullies? They can do or have something you don't so they pick on you for it, always wanting to feel and think like they are better than everyone else or they try to cover up their insecurities. They all to try to look cool so everyone can pay attention to them or laugh at their dumb jokes, so you can't see the simple fact of the matter is they either envy you or are just sad.*

Dametrix hated bullies. He watched W.D. and thought about stopping him and he almost didn't hear the bell ring. Everyone scattered like roaches into first period.

Somehow Stanly had a higher grade than the rest. Dametrix didn't know why. *Is he smart and plays dumb or just lucky and knows how to cheat?*

He always seemed to find a way of doing things. When Dametrix asked him how he had the highest grade in the class, even higher than Martino, who was a boy genius compared to the rest, he laughed that annoying smug laugh and said, "It's numbers son. I love money."

While sitting in class, Dametrix could feel someone staring at him. He looked around the class, at the walls filled with math posters and at the bookshelves, and then looked in the back at Stanly, who for once was quiet. Even the teacher, Mr. Gamaliel, was surprised.

Dametrix called out to him after class, "Stanly Iscariot, are you OK?"

He turned around and replied, "Hmm." Time went by and Dametrix stared at him and then he said, "It's my only favorite thing in school: lunchtime. After that, I don't care for the rest of the periods except for Mrs. Stephanie's class. I don't know what it is about her. Everyone has a hot teacher, and she is mine." Everyone in class laughed out loud.

When the final period bell rang Dametrix thought it wasn't a bad day. He watched documentaries in most of his classes and didn't have to run in p.e. Stanly walked over and stared at him while he was walking to the bus. He ignored him, thinking to himself he had something for him since he didn't want to listen.

 Later on that night, Dametrix dreamt he was looking around for something in a corn field with a worried look on his face, not sure if he was really in a dream or whether he was wide awake. A faded red farmhouse sat at a far distance in the middle of nowhere, but with a circle of grass and corn crops around it, you couldn't tell how far it was. He looked to the left of the farmhouse, then to the right. No roads or power lines to be seen. In the other circle of the cut field was just corn surrounding the house with a cut pathway leading from Dametrix to the house. With a creeping feeling running down his spine, he walked away from the red farmhouse's path onto the path of the cut corn leading away from the house.

He stared at how bright, yellow, and green the crops made everything look. Even the sun was vivid, making everything bright and detailed. A cool breeze waved the corn back and forth. Dametrix ran, and then jumped but fell to the ground face-first when he tried to fly. He failed several more times and grew angry. Suddenly he stopped and looked forward in front of him, seeing corn stalks standing tall as if they were a bunch of corn people looking down at him, standing in his way, waving back and forth. He thought about what David said. Unable to concentrate on how to fly, he was too worried about whether this was real or not, and if it was a dream.

He closed his eyes and the breeze turned into a wind. He felt as if the red farmhouse was behind him, slowly creeping up on him with its broken windows that looked like scary eyes and a front door for a mouth.

He said to himself, "Oh my God, I need to get out of here." He ran through the crops and the husks slapped his face with every step.

Left, right, front, back, top, bottom. He kept getting hit with them. He then jumped and shot up in the air. Opening his eyes while looking down, he saw the farmhouse clearly as if it was right behind him where he jumped. Wiping the pieces of corn silk from his face, he smiled and screamed, "Yeah! Woohoo!" Remembering how David waved his hand around, Dametrix lifted up his left hand and moved it around in a counterclockwise motion. With his eyes closed, thinking about the dream world, he felt something pulling him down hard. When he opened his eyes, he saw the ground coming at him fast against a cloud of smoke.

As the cloud cleared, Dametrix looked up and saw David standing in front of him with a pale, emotionless look on his face. He stood and hugged David. It was like David came back to life. "Hey dude, are you OK man?"

Dametrix smiled while mocking David. "Yeah bro, ha haha. Hey, do you want to go back to my friend's dream again?"

He replied "Sorry man, I can't. I don't have the energy since I overslept, and I exerted my spirit."

Dametrix looked at him weirdly since David never really used words like that before. After a few seconds, Dametrix replied, "Don't worry, I got this. I learned from the last time you kinda showed me. Just tell me what to do if
I mess up."

"Nah little man I can't do it today," David said, exasperated.

Dametrix scoffed. "You will be fine, let's go." He grabbed David's hand and flew off to the bar with the underground room.

DMT JOURNEYS

As they landed in front of the building, Dametrix looked at the entrance with the small revolving doors. The big sign on the building said The Bar. "So whose bright idea was it to name it that?"

David replied, "We all thought it was a simple, funny joke, so we never really tried to change it or ask questions."

Dametrix walked inside, listening to all the chatter of people talking. It was a huge room. Some of the women looked like princesses. Others looked like knights. Any popular movie or cartoon character he had seen was being portrayed by someone in the room. He looked back and David was standing outside with that same expression as before on his face.

"Comes on man, let's go," David said.

Dametrix shouted, "Hey, where's the secret dark room?" Everyone immediately got quiet and stared at him. David covered his mouth and rushed off with Dametrix into another room. "Are you serious man? You can't just yell that out!"

A big robot-looking character dressed up in a suit of armor with a long rifle on his back walked up to them.

Seeing this, Dametrix smiled. "Oh I love that game. I get it, you're Master!"

"Shhhhh!" David said. The man in the suit of armor looked down at him and asked in a calm Mexican-American accent, "Is this one with you, David?"

"Yeah man, that's my friend Dametrix. He's new here, don't mind him."

The man reached out his hand, which was covered with metallic green armor with a little light flashing on it. "Nice to meet you man, I'm Gilbert. A friend of David's is a friend of mine. I'll show you to the room, but you can't be shouting stuff, especially after what you guys pulled last time. You know how hard it was to get rid of the watcher. Plus you never know who's listening. Some people here try to run back and talk to the Watchers snitching. I don't know why, but I'm guessing they're hoping to get some reward or special treatment for trying to be on their good side, I guess. Follow me, I'll lead you to it."

They walked up to a bald guy with red marking that ran from his head to along his body and seemed to go around him, with two blades on his back with an ax. He stood in a booth. The guy in the armor reached out his hand and they fist bumped up, down, and side-to-side then opened up their fingers like imitating an explosion, twiddled their fingers together, then closed their hands in the shape of a mouth, tapped each other's palm and said, "Feed the chicken."

Standing aside, Gilbert said, "There you go homies, enjoy."

David was hesitant but Dametrix grabbed him and pulled him in. "Are you ready?" He floated upward with

David hanging on to him again. They looked at all the cool colors sparkling as they floated around, heading straight for Stanly's house.

It was a bright, sunny day. A pool with clear water was splashing from left to right. A little black bird landed on Stanly's stomach while he floated in a red inflatable donut with red shorts on.

"Hey cute little bird," Stanly called, "what's good with you?"

The bird's black eyes turned red. "Who are you calling cute, boy?"

The bird growled. Stanly, shocked, said, "Oh no, not again. Ah sh—" The bird grew, forty feet tall and pushed Stanly to the bottom of the pool, nearly crushing him with its feet. Water splashed everywhere as Stanly quickly tried to swim away. The bird grabbed him with its feathery wings and lifted Stanly up to its mouth. Stanly realized what it was about to do. "Wait, wait! Don't eat me please, I'll do anything."

The bird opened its huge, black beaks. "I've heard that before. You had one job and I told you I would be back for you if you failed." "Fine I'll do it, Dutch, please just don't eat me! I'll tell Dametrix, I'm sorry!" The bird lowered him into its mouth. Stanly screamed louder, "OK, and I wet the bed!" The bird swallowed him. While Stanly screamed as he was falling down the bird's throat, the bird realized something was up. "Wait, what's going on? This isn't supposed to happen!" Stanly fell farther and farther while flapping his arm around and yelling, seeing nothing but darkness.

He opened his eyes and quickly got up in his bed, covered in sweat. For a moment, he saw a dark figure, but he rubbed his eyes and it disappeared.

Waking up suddenly, Dametrix looked at the time. At first, he was worried, thinking he was late, but was relieved to see what time it was. Five a.m. He thought about Stanly. He lay back down wondering what happened. He wasn't trying to eat him. Then, he thought about how Stanly always dreamt about sunny days or relaxing. At first, Dametrix almost thought maybe he could control his dreams. They always seemed to be great dreams. Dametrix figured maybe Stanly's dreams would be darker or he would have regrets for robbing people. But no, he really had no regrets about it.

Dametrix stayed in bed until he had to get ready for school. He decided to wear blue jeans and a black shirt with Bob Marley laughing and a bird symbol on it. While he waited at the bus stop, Martino showed up first as always then came Stanly. He stared at me and Sam. He was always the last to show up besides Dametrix, but today Dametrix was the first. Unlike last time, he woke up early and still ended up late. He yelled out. He didn't even know how that was possible.

Martino's first words to Dametrix were, "Wow, you're here early. That's a first."

"I see you're picking up on your best friend, Stanly slick mouth," Dametrix said. Martino laughed nervously.

He shouted out "Hey, he isn't my best friend, you are buddy," and quickly put his hand over his mouth, realizing that Stanly was right next to him. He was wearing a black shirt with writing that said "Please keep your mouth closed. I don't want to catch your stupid."

Dametrix laughed hysterically while looking at Martino with his button up shirt all the way to his neck and black skinny jeans. It looked like the shirt was choking him. You could tell his step-parents pick out his clothes. They were screaming "Pull your pants up!"

"Don't try to be like that other one." Dametrix grabbed little Martino with his hand around his little head and messed up his curly hair. "I can't be mad at you. You're like my little brother."

As the school bus pulled up, they could hear the squeaking from the driver hitting the brakes. Everyone got inside and sat down. Dametrix could feel someone looking at him and when he turned around, he saw the person was Stanly. He then asked Martino to sit next to him. He was so happy, unlike Sam, who had to sit next to Stanly. This time, he didn't bug him with questions or anything. Even

Sam noticed it. "What's good man, you OK son?"

Stanly said with a fake smile "Yup," while staring at Dametrix the whole time.

Dametrix and Stanly had two periods together, math and economics, and Martino was in math class with them. That was the only class they had together. Sam and Dametrix had physical education and ROTC, of course. He just needed some elective to pass in every class. Everyone asked Dametrix what was wrong with him, even the economics teacher, Mr. Enoch. Everyone said his class wasn't that important and they were thinking about taking it out of the school, which Dametrix disagreed with. Mr. Enoch seemed to be a very educated person to him. After class, the teacher said to him, "Stanly seems to be behaving abnormally. It's intriguing and obscure… perhaps the parentals presented an obstacle? Theoretically feasible allocution extraneous to the situation."

Dametrix stared at him, flustered, and thought to himself, *Why couldn't you just say Stanly is acting strange or different? Is it an issue at home with his parents? You should talk to him to try to cheer him up about something none relating to the subject of the matter.*

Wait, I understood that. I never get why I always understand his big, sophisticated words.

Dametrix smiled and said, "OK, Mr. Enoch."

As they headed back to the bus, Dametrix was about to talk to Stanly and ask what was wrong, but Stanly approached first, saying "I know it was you, and I have something to tell you."

Dametrix didn't know what he was talking about, then he smiled, and it all came back to him. *I can't believe he's going to do it! I'm laughing inside. Should I let him continue or stop him? Nah, that laugh of his... ugh, and all the things he said to me. With his mean little jokes, now it's his turn to get laughed at.* Dametrix tried to hold in his laugh. "Yesss," he replied.

He looked at him with an angry, yet powerless expression. "I wet the bed; yup that's it."

"Are you sure that's it?" Stanly looked embarrassed. Dametrix felt like it was kind of dumb to continue but he didn't care, he wanted all the cake for himself. He hated that expression. He squinted his eyes.

"Why you ask, Dutch Dametrix," he said with a smile on his face. "Did a little birdy tell you something?" Dametrix couldn't help chuckling. "No."

"Teach me how you did it," he said angrily. "I know you have been studying dreams, especially after your nightmare. Did you forget I was the one that told you to go search it up, son? And you used to tell us about your dreams until you got butt hurt and stopped. So come on, kid, tell me," he demanded with his strong, ghetto New York accent.

Oh my gosh, what have I done to myself?

The whole ride home he continuously asked the same thing. Of course, God had to get a laugh out of this.

Dametrix was usually the third person to get dropped off. With his bad luck, the bus driver was sick, and they had another driver who took everyone home first but him. Stanly's stop approached and he told the driver a sob story, then said, "No I'm going to his house."

"Why?"

"So you can show me how to do it! I won't stop asking you until you agree to show me. So, how do you do it? How do you do it?" He kept repeating the question for the whole ride until Dametrix's stop came. He was so happy to get off the bus, but Stanly followed him.

While walking home fast, all he could hear was Stanly asking and begging. Dametrix started running home, but he was right behind him. Dametrix forgot how fast Stanly could run, probably because he'd been running from the cops his whole teenage life. He was running so hard his books were moving up and down in his book bag, hurting his lower back.

Dametrix reached home, disappointed to see the empty parking space right next to the house. He scoffed. *If only Grandma was here, damn it, she's never here.* He stopped to grab his keys as Stanly got closer, but the keys fell. It felt like he was in a horror film. This would have been the part where he died because Stanly popped up right behind him.

He turned around and Dametrix yelled, "Fine, OK, I'll show you, just shut up!"

A big grin appeared on his face. "Why do you always want to do it the hard way? You know I always win." he said cockily as he walked inside the house with a smug look on his face. "OK, first, take a shower – you can use my bathroom."

"Oh, is this the first important step?"

"No, you're dirty from doing all that running. These are new sheets."

As he took a shower, Dametrix pulled his rolling chair closer to the bed and held his dream journal. *How am I even going to show him how to do it? It took me a while – like a month – to learn how to do it. And it just spontaneously happened. David helped and showed me how to finish it.*

I guess I'll look up the info again online, tell him not to get his hopes up, and just fake it until I can meet up with David and ask him.

Stanly came out of the shower about to put on his shirt. Dametrix noticed all the bruise marks, cuts and scratches on his body. With an intense look, Stanly said, "God puts people in situations to test them. I'm not going to be a failure even if I have to cheat."

DMT JOURNEYS

Stanly had never talked like that before. Maybe he was angry at God. *I guess I was wrong and never knew as much as I thought I did. Am I wrong for not hanging out with him as I used to? He changed so much, taking what he learned from me the wrong way. Now he seems to be getting way out of control. Is it my fault?*

At that moment, Dametrix felt badly for him and started to understand why he always wanted to hang out with the rest of his friends. *He's probably lonely and doesn't want to do things but feels that he's being tested and has to do bad things.*

"Alright buddy," Dametrix began, "let's teach you how to control your dream. First, you must go to sleep and when you sleep after thirty minutes, I'm going to wake you and you have to tell me what you dreamed about. We have a bottle of sleeping pills and cough medicine I took from Grandma's room since she works at the hospital. She has all the best and strong stuff. If it really gets that difficult, we'll just use the chloroform." *I am going to try and do this the fastest way possible.*

Using his phone, Dametrix timed him with every try. He thought Stanly would get worse for a beginner, but he actually became better. The first time he was woken, he was yelling and screaming. Then the second time, he kicked in his sleep. It felt creepy but funny watching him sleep. The third time he woke up by himself. He said he was already aware of his dreams and tried to turn on the lights and fly. After a couple more tries, he woke up on his own with a smile "I know how to control my dreams," he said.

After explaining, Dametrix was surprised and jealous at the same time. How did he learn to fly already on his first couple of tries and all within five hours? He wondered if Stanly was lying. Or maybe he just didn't want to seem like a failure, so he was faking it. "OK," Dametrix said, "show me." There was only a little bit of stuff left – Dametrix was surprised Stanly didn't overdose from all the pills.

Taking the last bit of stuff left, even mixing it, Dametrix fell asleep on the couch and he woke up next to that creepy farmhouse again in the cornfield. He started running fast and screamed, "No, no, no, no!" as he jumped in the air and flew off. *Why aren't I at my dream home?* He moved his hand clockwise, thinking of his dream home. "This has to work! If this newbie can control his dream that fast, I better be able to master it."

He stared hard and concentrated and a portal opened. "Yes!" It pulled him in and it felt like a roller coaster. He moved up, down, and around, spiraling. It then sent him flying towards his house. He crashed and then tried to get up, thinking, "I'm glad this was all a dream 'cause Grandma would kill me if I broke through the roof."

He looked around and it was dark again. He couldn't even see the stairs this time. Instead, he felt them with his left hand, which meant the kitchen was on his right side. Suddenly he felt a cold chill down his spine and quickly turned but saw nothing. Then he felt a tap on his right shoulder. He froze. He heard a growling, like a big wolf from the scary movies, then a soft noise whispering, "I told you I was coming for you."

Trying to imagine a gun, he was so frightened, but then a sword appeared in his hand. A tall monster glowing with sharp, pointy teeth roared toward him and he ran, crashing out the living room window and out of the house.

He got up and threw the sword towards it. It went right over the monster's shoulder. "What the hell, man, you almost killed me! Wait, can you even die in the dream world?" Then, he heard that laugh. A gun appeared in his hand and he pointed it. "I'm going to kill you, monster."

The beast raised its hands, saying "Whoa, hold on, it's me."

"No, I don't know any monster so you're going to die and if you die in my dreams it means I'm going to kill you for real cause your mind makes it real. And we all know you can't live without the mind."

The monster gave a confused look and said, "Hey, you stole that from the ma."

Dametrix laughed. "It's been a long time. When we laugh like this reminds me how we met and the stuff we did together before things changed." Dametrix noticed that his laugh didn't annoy him. He then transformed into a bald man with glasses wearing a long leather coat. "Take the red pill or the blue pill. We both said it was one of the greatest movies ever." Then Dametrix was wearing a black coat with a Guy Fawkes mask. He remembered one of their old sayings: "We have to control our dreams and don't let our dreams control us."

He stopped laughing and looked around with a serious look on his face. Dametrix looked at his hands and wondered how he was able to make a gun appear from nothing. *How did we end up here?* He assumed they would have ended up at their dream house or dream world. "Why are you looking around?"

He said "I feel something in my stomach. Like something is coming, like I've felt this before but it's different."

"What do you mean by 'what you've felt before'?"

A figure walked towards them. "I know that walk," Dametrix said. "Hold on, don't go. It's cool man. I know this guy, that's the one I want you to meet. David, over here!"

He quickly disappeared, then Dametrix felt a force with dark red eyes pushing towards him. It had a familiar cold touch. David suddenly appeared in front of him.

"Oh, hey dude." Dametrix looked at him as he stared at me with droopy red but tired eyes with bags underneath them. Concerned, he said, "Are you OK, man? You seem a little different." Then he heard a shot fired at them and they both ducked. David's eyes turned red with an angry expression on his face. He showed his teeth as if he were going to growl.

"Stanly, this is David," Dametrix said. "He's the one that showed me how to do all of this."

Stanly walked towards them and stared at David like he was staring at Dametrix earlier on the bus. David reached out his left hand. "Oh, hey man," he said. He had a long sleeve covering his entire arm, which Dametrix thought was weird because he always wore a hippie tie-dyed kind of shirt with lots of colors and blue pants with his curly hair hanging around his shoulders. Now he had on a black, long-sleeve shirt with black pants. His hair floated upward like he was underwater or touching a Van De Graaff generator.

The only thing Stanly could say was "'Sup?"

Dametrix hit Stanly with his arm. "Don't be rude! He's the one that can teach us all about this stuff."

Stanly whispered, "This weird creepy looking white boy, he looks like he works at Hot Topic."

"OK, that's enough. Are you sure you're OK, David?"

David nodded. "Yeah little man it's just my mom being a little sick so I'm helping her out."

Stanly quickly replied, "Where do you stay?"

Dametrix looked at him like "What are you up to? You better not be trying to rob him."

David said, "I stay in Brooklyn."

Stanly replied, "Oh, that's where I'm from," and reached out his hand with a smile on his face. They shook hands. Stanly asked, "What's your name again, B?" He said, "David." Stanly said "David what? I'm Stanly Iscariot."

"I'm David Haman. I like the outfit, dude. That's my favorite movie, too. I even like the last one. Those are awesome movies."

Dametrix watched them laughing and joking, unamused. "OK, best buddies, can we get a move on? You can show us how to get into people's dreams."

David said, "Sorry little dude. I have to go. You know how to do it. You can show him, just take him to dream world. Meet up with Gilbert, I think he should be there."

He walked, and then flew off. Stanley watched him and then said, "OK, let's go then," and grabbed Dametrix. Dametrix started to yell, feeling someone shaking him.

Waking up seeing Stanley staring at him. Then he went on the computer and started to type.

"Yo, what's your problem? Why are you acting weirder than usual? Why did you wake me? I didn't even show you the dream world!" He shushed him. Dametrix stared at him.

"Come here come look at this," Stanly said. He moved over to the laptop and looked at a website to search for people and saw the name David Haman in the search bar. "Oh my gosh, really Stanly? The guy clearly said he doesn't want to hang out!"

Stanly smiled and said "If I listened to what people say as much as you do, I would be a gullible loser like you. Besides, have you ever known me to not do something people tell me not to do?"

"That's invading his privacy and pretty stalker-ish," Dametrix argued. "There's probably hundreds of Davids in Brooklyn. How are you going to even find him?"

"Well lucky me, there's only two Davids by that name in Brooklyn which fits his description. He couldn't be younger than us or that much older from the age he told me no more than twenty-five."

Dametrix looked at the website incredulously. "Wait, what? Damn it! Why does God always give you luck? Meanwhile, me, who tries to do all the right things, gets bad luck."

"That doesn't mean that it's him. Only one way to find out, let's go!"

He grabbed Dametrix and they ran outside. "It's nine in the morning. How are we even going to get there on a Saturday?" Dametrix said.

"Simple. I used the Uber app on my phone and got a ride. I did that the moment I woke up since I knew I was going to find him by then." Just as Stanly spoke, the car pulled up. Stanly grabbed his book bag.

Wow, he really planned all of this out, from fake talking to David to calling for the ride. Dametrix watched Stanly, who was scrolling through websites on his phone. *Why does he get caught for the little crime, but never the big ones? Does it even really matter? He always gets out free with a slap on the wrist. That kid is a real menace to society. He's going to be trouble when he grows up.*

They arrived at the somewhat upper-middle-class area in Brooklyn. Dametrix could tell because the streets were clean, and the neighbors were outside watering their lawns. *Who even does that except for rich people with a lot of time on their hands? Our neighbors are nice but they always have guns on them. Or just look like the type to not mess with.*

They knocked on the door and an Indian guy opened it, wearing khaki pants and a white t-shirt. Stanly scowled because he hated that brand of t-shirt. Then Stanly smiled, opened his mouth with the most proper, no-slang-in-hissentence voice, and said, "Hi there sir, we are looking for our best friend. We think he moved; his name is David
Haman. We are so worried about him."

The man looked confused. "Sorry kids, there is no David here."

They said goodbye. Stanly flipped him off, then opened his bag and pulled out a jar with small holes on the top, releasing some bugs underneath the house in a hole he dug. They walked back to the car.

"Do you always walk around with stuff like that in your bag?" Dametrix said.

"You always have to have back up plans. Trust me, that guy is a tyrant, he deserves it."

They next visited a hospital. Stanly walked up to a woman at the front desk and said, "Hi, we're looking for our best buddy, David Haman" again with that fake voice of his. We heard he was in here and were so worried and concerned about him."

The woman said, "Sure, I can help you find him. Just need some IDs."

"His mom asked us to come. She's such a nice lady."

The woman said, "He's in room QS 1092."

They walked toward the room and Dametrix thought about why David might be in the hospital. *He never told me that. Maybe he told Stanly. And why does Stanly have IDs of me and him? He looked at me and said, man, always prepare for the worst. Hoping you are the best of the worst.*

But that's not how it goes. I think I know why I stopped hanging out with him.

It seemed the plastic, sick smell got stronger the further they went down the hallway after taking the elevator.

It also grew quieter. At the door to the room I stared inside while Stanly ran in and said to me, "Hey, you're going to want to see this."

His heart raced as he slowly walked in. He could not believe what he saw nor knew what to think.

It was David lying in a bed and strapped to machines that seemed like they were monitoring him. Dametrix blurted out, "What the hell is this?"

Stanly replied while looking at a clipboard, "It's a machine, stupid. Says here he's in a coma."

Dametrix grabbed one of the chairs and sat down. *Why didn't he tell me he was in a coma?* Stanly stared at David in his hospital gown, sheets over him, and listened to the machine beeps. Stanly then said, "Don't worry, on the chart it said it's a semi-coma."

He stood against the wall, took twenty deep breaths, and said, "Come hold my throat so you can knock me out. Dametrix always wanted a chance to knock Stanly out."

Dametrix was so shocked he couldn't get out of the chair. Stanly then sat on one of the chairs, then took a pill while sniffing a rag in a paper bag.

"Wait, where did you get that?" Right after Dametrix asked the question Stanly passed out. Dametrix then took three pills, figuring it would work faster than inhaling the rag.

The hospital room was now darker and cold. Dametrix was looking around when something suddenly grabbed him he yelp Stanly said, "OK let's enter his dream, scary cat hurry."

Dametrix gave him a strange look "Why the big rush?"

Stanly replied, "Because hospitals normally have lots of demons or ghosts wandering around. It's the next best thing to a cemetery. I was on this website called allnurses where they would explain the things they have seen Now hurry before something finds us."

Dametrix sighed and said, "Really with your conspiracy theory again!"

Stanly replied, "No stupid, just because it's a theory doesn't mean it's not real. A lot of things have been discovered based on theories. The term conspiracy theory is a CIA made name for uptight, dumb people like you to belittle people who think beyond what they are programmed to believe. The whole laws of gravity started on theory. It's even in the damn name. People thought the world was flat long ago and would laugh at you if you said the world was a sphere. Now it's vice versa. What is magic but unexplained science? Open your eyes. I'm not saying everything you read is true on the web, but do you really think it's all fake and you're the only thing in existence besides the millions of organisms on earth? You're that simpleminded to think that the whole damn universe was just created for only you? Not including the millions of other planets, what the hell are they there for? Just to look pretty you morons. Now, when you say you saw an alien, it's not as crazy as it was before. There's some truth to this stuff." I mean just freaking look. You are Astro projecting. I understand people fear the truth but don't be dumb to it."

"OK, fine, you win. Answer me this, Mr. Know It All How are we even here?" Dametrix said. "It was harder last time."

He replied, "I think there's strange energy here, or maybe even at all hospitals. Probably due to so much death and people who come here, some who were witches or cursed. They carry a strong spiritual field with them and you know hospitals, they never lose power. It makes the energy stronger. Which attracts most spirits that feed on them.

"You always have people dying or waking up from death, so there's a lot of spiritual activity going on. There's probably a spirit net here so the dead can't easily run away. I think that's why we didn't leave here or go to the dream world."

Dametrix was dumbfounded. *How does he know all that stuff? If I wasn't astral projecting next to him I would have just thought it's all fake conspiracy BS. Half of what he told me, David had to explain it to me but he knew it down to the fact that there are creatures that feed on energy. David just called them night ghouls or dream ghouls.*

"Come on hurry," he said and Dametrix snapped out of it.

They entered David's dream. It was different than when Dametrix did it with Stanly. His was like entering a portal going to the dream world except this one was dark at the end of it. Dametrix quickly put his hands over his mouth while watching David hover over a little kid who was maybe eleven or twelve, lying in bed surrounded by paintings and drawings on a wall that had the word kain written on it. As a clear light was being absorbed in his spirit body, the kid struggled to move back and forth, similar to sleeping.

Dametrix pushed David and he stared at him with malicious red eyes. His teeth were sharp. He was shocked Stanly just shot him in the shoulder. He said, "Damn I miss floating towards him. The kid woke up. Dametrix put his finger over his mouth. "Shhh." David floated out of the house with Stanly quickly following him. "Come back here, David," Stanly yelled. "We just want to talk."

"I knew there was something weird about you," David said angrily, trying to get up from falling as he held his shoulder and walked. Trying to fly jump and fly Stanly yelled, "I guess criminals can sense another criminal." Dametrix followed them and thought about how this could be. *Stanly met the guy in five minutes and figured him out. I spent hours with him and did not realize anything. Am I really that gullible like everyone else in society in my little bubble?*

He screamed, "It's not real, it's just another conspiracy theory. The government is protecting me, but we don't even trust or really like the government, so how could we trust it so blindly?"

When it comes to scary stuff, we are so quick to hide away from it behind false realities being spoon fed to us, just like a little kid hiding behind our parents. The parent that steals and lies to us, that sees us as just a helpless object afraid of the truth. Is Stanly right that we are just numbers? I see stuff like this in movies but just dismissed it as such. So many lies to dumb us down, making us lazy and oblivious while making us feel good about ourselves. Isn't that what everyone says? I love my country and city as much as the next guy, even more so, but I'm not going to let it happen again before it's too late. Fool me once.

Dametrix yelled and flew towards David and grabbed him. He threw him and they landed in another house and another kid's room, Dametrix lifted him up in the air with one hand. "Enough! All this time you lied to me, why?" He slammed him against the wall. Dametrix slammed him into the wall harder each time but he couldn't phase through it; instead he crashed into it. A cup on the dresser of a nearby bed moved with every slam.

David reverted into what he previously looked like when Dametrix first saw him. One bang, his black shirt changed to a tie-dyed shirt. Two bangs and his arms changed, three bangs and the cup fell off the dresser onto the floor. The kid on the bed next to the dresser jumped up wearing his Pokemon pajamas and stared at the wall as if he could see them.

David yelled, "I'm sorry man, I didn't know I was changing into a ghoul. I was just going to take a little energy. I didn't want to die. I didn't mean to take your energy."

A tear rolled out of his eye and Dametrix loosened his grip. "At first, I didn't want to be alive cause it was so much better in the dream world. But after what you said to me about growing up. I started thinking you're right, growing up and dying is natural and going to come whether you want it to or not. You should just enjoy your time you have alive and have great memories making the right choices to better yourself and people around you. If you live a good life, then, you shouldn't have anything to worry about when you die.

"I started missing my mom and heard her cry at my bed. I wanted to wake up, but I couldn't. I didn't know how to. I couldn't ask you because I didn't want to tell you I was the one that stupidly put myself in a coma cause... I tried to kill myself." Dametrix looked at David, shocked. "All because I was a coward and didn't want to face life and the inevitable head-on. It took a fifteen-year-old to make me realize that. Life is worth living and is what you make of it. If poor people or people who suffer every day push through it, not give up, and make something of themselves in the future sometimes, why can't I?"

"Maybe we can help you wake up," Dametrix said as he looked at Stanly next to him. Stanly gave him a weird look and replied, "What the hell are you looking at me for? Do I look like an angel? What do you want me to do?"

Dametrix smiled as he put David down. "What does your conspiracy theory say about bringing people out of comas?

"Oh sure, now let's all depend on the one you called crazy to get us out of this."

"Dametrix yelled, "Well?" Stanly shrugged his shoulders, "I don't know. Isn't this the part in every movie or TV show where you wake up after you have an epiphany?"

Dametrix rolled his eyes and looked at David. "OK I have a plan if you need the energy to wake up. How about we give you just the right amount of energy where your spirit is still tired but it's not at the brink of becoming a ghoul then someone has to stand outside and give you energy to wake you up out of your sleep at the right time.

"Just follow my lead. I'm going to give him some energy in here. You get out of his dream which should take you back to the hospital due to your dream state connection to your body. See I did some reading myself. And try to wake him up by giving his body energy since you're good at waking people up."

Stanly looked at him, confused. "Don't worry about it, just wait for me outside his dream and I'll tell you what to do." Stanly nodded and flew back to the hospital while Dametrix gave him energy as they held hands. David said, "When will I know to stop or let go?"

"I'll let you know," Dametrix said. David began to glow and Dametrix fell to his knees. "OK you can let go now." David let go reluctantly. "Let's fly back to your body and meet up with Stanly."

"Thank you so much, Dametrix I appreciate you. It's not so hard to fly now and I don't feel hungry. I actually feel like this is going to work."

When they reached the hospital, they looked at Stanly's spirit getting off the floor.

"What happened to you dude?" Dametrix said.

Stanly got up, wheezing and panting. "Doesn't matter, let's go get out of here."

Dametrix grabbed Stanly's hands and David lied down on his body as they both put their hands on him. The lights in the hospital started to flicker. They heard a growling sound. Stanly said, "Hurry up, wake him up now.'' The noise grew closer and louder. Suddenly there was a white blast and Stanly woke up from his dream state. Dametrix opened his eyes to Stanly shaking and slapping him and telling him to wake up.

"I'm up, I'm up – stop shaking me." He smiled and slapped me again.

He rushed to David and his eyes opened. As he opened his mouth, Dametrix slapped him really hard in the face.

He yelled "Ow! What you do that for?"

"Just returning the favor."

A tear fell from his eyes as he slowly got up. "I said don't get up, your muscles haven't been used yet." He smiled. "The best movie ever. Thanks, man. I can't wait to see my mom again. I know she will be so happy."

On their way out into the hallway, they met a lady who passed right by them wearing a nurse's outfit. Then they heard a scream and a loud noise. They heard David saying "Don't cry Mom, get up. Yes, it's really me, I'm here for you now. I won't leave you ever again."

Stanly remained distant after that. Dametrix didn't know if he was mad and continued practicing lucid dreaming. Stanly stopped asking if they could hang out.

It felt like he couldn't go into dream world or dream house anymore, but it would seem school got in the way for him anyway. He didn't want to bug Stanly, who said he was just going home to do homework.

There was talk of Sam going to boot camp but Dametrix didn't know how true it was. Sam was always going somewhere.

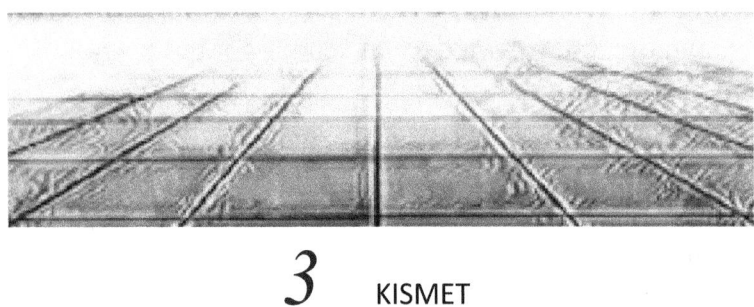

3   KISMET

Dametrix opened his eyes and looked around, seeing a sunny day. He stood in a grassy field feeling the cool breeze. The sweet smell of grass was in the air and a mountain peak in the distance was surrounded with dark clouds. A man yelled from a far distance. He fixated on how this dream felt so vivid. As the sound got louder so did the sound of horses galloping.

He coughed from the dust cloud, which broke his concentration. Dametrix opened his eyes to see a man sitting on a black horse with all white hair wearing shining armor like a knight would wear. "Sir, do you hear me?" The man said. Dametrix's jaw dropped slightly. "Whoa!" said the man to the horses. Dametrix watched the man get off the horse and stand tall, towering over him. "Sir, do you hear me? Can ye not speaketh? I am King Everest. What is thy nameth, younker?"

Raising the visor over his face and looking at Dametrix, King Everest was a young, brown-eyed man with black hair. Dametrix made a weird face and body gestures like a baby who was trying to speak or yell. "Sir, are you OK?" King Everest asked, concerned. He swiftly slapped Dametrix hard on the face. It made a loud noise from the metal gauntlet Everest was wearing. Dametrix opened his mouth wide and yelled with tears coming from his eyes. The horses let out a loud "neigh" as if both of them were laughing.

King Everest burst into laughter too. "Pardon me, I don't mean to laugh." Everest chuckled to Dametrix as Dametrix just stared at him angrily. "I did need that good laugh for it might be my last..." He looked towards the sky, a hint of sadness in his eyes. "Please excuse me, I have to be on my way." He stopped to get on his horse before looking at Dametrix again. He had one foot in the saddle and was about to climb up.

Dametrix came a little closer and placed his hand on the king's shoulder. "Where are you going?"

"I'm on my way to the top of that mountain to slay a dragon. Legend has it the beast lives in a castle that was built for a king with an excessive appetite. He believed the creature could be controlled. Had his workers build the castle up above that mountain, which I was told was

29,029 feet to protect all the treasures stolen from destroyed kingdoms and the precious beast that helped him defeat his enemies.

"Greed finally caught up to him when the creature turned on him. Since he was so high up, no one could come in time to help him. He ran around and hid, waiting for his troops to respond to the signal he sent. By the time the troops arrived, it was too late. The only things found were leftover ruins of the king and the hidden beast waiting for them. The majority, if not all of those troops, met the same fate as their king. Many have tried to slay the beast. Some to get the treasure, others to stop it from eating the feast it has when it flies down attacking villages. All have failed. Those who do make it past the treacherous weather don't make it past the beast. Now the evil thing turns on my kingdom and is terrorizing my people."

King Everest huffed as he got back on the black horse. "While on the horse the king positioned himself saying, "The armor is a bit of a nuisance." He looked at the mountain. Sitting up straight, trying to look proud and brave like a true knight, he said, "It was a pleasure meeting you, Sir..No Name."

Dametrix looked around then, realizing the king was alone. "Hold on. Where is your army? Doesn't every king have one?"

"Well sir, if thou must knoweth, I ordered them not to follow. That vile beast has killed enough of my people, scaring all the women, families, bairns, and parents." The king grunted, "It just makes me incredibly angry. Why must there be destruction and death?"

Dametrix looked at him. "I'll help you and we'll take care of this together."

"Are you mad? Didn't you hear what I said!"

"Yeah, dragon bad, kill it good, do you want me to help your people or not? Because I'm not taking no for an answer."

"Either you're mad, brave, or a fool."

With a smile, Dametrix replied, "You didn't bring an army and you're alone. I guess I'm whatever you are."

A flustered look came upon King Everest's face. "Shouldn't you be getting home? Where are thy parents bearn they must be worried sick."

"Don't worry, they're dead."

"Oh, I'm sorry to hear that."

"Is that extra horse for me? Thanks, I never rode one before."

"No, it's for Sir Radhanath and George! They will aid me in my quest," the king explained.

Ignoring what King Everest was saying, Dametrix grabbed the saddle of the white horse and jumped on and grabbed the rope connected to the bridle. "Let's see how they did it in the movies," Dametrix said, hurriedly riding off and leaving the other horse behind. "You can get your friends if you want, but that's going to waste too much time. That's a big mountain and the castle is at the peak."

Dametrix kicked the horse with the heel of his right boot and yelled "Yah!" The horse turned to the side, scowled at Dametrix, and took off full speed towards the mountain. King Everest looked at the smoke and the debris left behind and laughed, saying to himself, "Yup, he's a mad fool."

Dametrix was bouncing up and down and side to side, trying to hang on for his life. "Oh my gosh, why did I get myself into this?!" Dametrix yelled. "Whoa horsey, are you angry? I...am...so...sor...ry!" *I don't want to die! Wait, this is my dream. I got this.* He got into a crouching monkey position, hung on to the rope, and yelled "Hee-haw!"

Now there was a great distance between them both. King Everest tried, but he could not keep up. Instead, he fell more behind. Darkness closed in. All he could hear was the horse galloping, rocks falling, grumbling, and snow crunching on the ground. He was barely able to see in front of him as rigorous winds pushed against him with great force like they were trying to push him back. With snow everywhere, the mountain appeared to be covered in a white blanket. Dametrix led the way, seemingly guided by gut feeling, yelling with excitement. Suddenly, the sound stopped and all they could hear was the wind howling.

"I wonder why I couldn't speak earlier," Dametrix thought. "That was unusual. Am I able to still fly? I'll just fly away with the horse."

He got off the horse, reached over, and touched its underbelly. The scowl reappeared on the horse's face with a neigh and it kicked its front legs up a little higher. Dametrix fell to the ground. "OK fine, such a stubborn horse. Is it because I kicked you? I said sorry. I don't need this. I could just fly away and leave you."

He jumped multiple times and fell on his face, looking back and seeing the horse staring at him and neighing every time he failed, as if the horse were laughing at him.

He got up frustrated and walked towards the horse, which made a noise like it didn't want him to get on. "OK, since you look so sad making a noise like that, I'll just ride you again, right buddy?" As he reached up to get back on the horse, it took off. He chased it and just as he caught up to it he fell in the deep snow. "OK come back," Dametrix yelled. "I'm sorry, can I please ride you again?"

The horse moved in front of him neighing and showed its teeth. "Yeah, yeah, shut up," Dametrix said while getting on. They continued onwards, going faster until the horse just stopped, causing Dametrix to flip forward and roll onto the ground.

When he stood up he was staring at a dark, dilapidated castle that suddenly appeared in front of him, covered in ice. Dametrix walked up to the door and yelled, "Knock knock!" With a hard push, he kicked it open and exclaimed, "This is Dametrix!" *Bam!*

The seemingly frozen, rickety door burst open with a screech. Icicles fell as the door slammed behind him and stayed slightly ajar. He walked around and yelled, "Yooooo-hooooo! Where are you, dragon? Come here, boy!" He clapped his hands. "Let's get some exercise!"

He whistled while scanning the room but was barely able to see anything except for a dim light coming from the door, a couple of swords hanging on the wall, and what appeared to be skulls and bones on the floor from unfortunate knights. Slowly watching his step and not staying too far from the front door, Dametrix stayed on high alert, listening for any sound.

Red eyes suddenly appeared, then bright red teeth. After seemingly floating right after it, a dark red light shot up coming from the floor and traveled fast up to the red eyes. Then a roar with a fire blast came after it. Dametrix jumped out of the way and ran away from the front door.

King Everest got to the castle and saw the white horse a few feet away from the door. He walked slowly to the front door to only see fire shoot out the door, pushing the king and making him fly back to the snow. The door shut. Snow knocked loose from the castle fell onto the door, putting out most of the fire.

"No!" King Everest screamed. "Ye dumb, mad fool! You're not even wearing any armor, just strange clothing. I don't want any more people dying because of me, especially not a bairn." He looked around and found a rock. Everest grabbed it and started hitting the door while shouting and hoping he could make a dent big enough for him to fit his sword through.

Inside, Dametrix hid behind a big column and panted hard. "This is kinda fun. Scary as hell, but fun."

The dragon's heavy footsteps make loud thumping noises like drums. Fire spread on curtains around the wall, lighting up the room. Dametrix peeked over to the left and now got a better view of the tall, black, slim, scaly dragon. The tail slid on the floor as the creature moved around the castle looking for him. On his right side, he saw a glowing object. Squinting his eyes to see better, he realized it was a sword. He took a deep breath and grabbed it.

The dragon heard his footsteps and turned around, breathing fire towards him. Dametrix ran quickly to the right, screaming "Hot hot hot!" He then jumped into a hole in the wall and quickly got up and away from fire shooting out of it. After the fire fizzled out, he leaned towards the hole to take a look. He saw the crystal-like, smooth red eyes looking back. He smiled nervously then ran away. As the walls fell behind him, roars bellowed, overpowering the space around him.

"Why am I running straight?" Dametrix thought out loud. He turned left as the dragon continued smashing walls and he brushed off the rubble. "Ha, stupid creature." The dragon stopped running. Dametrix looked to the left and sighed. "Oh, come on! How the hell did you hear that? No one ever said dragons had good hearing." He searched for the sword.

When he found the shining sword, he faced the dragon's terrifying, red eyes as it got closer to him.

Boom, boom, boom. The same rhythm continued as King Everest kept hitting the door with the rock. He finally made a big hole the size of a fist. He looked and saw Dametrix pressed up against the wall. "I'm coming, you brave fool! Go hide somewhere," he yelled.

Dametrix looked at the bright light coming from the hole. Seeing a head-shaped shadow, he smiled then ran towards the dragon. A surprised look came on the dragon's face. It opened its mouth, the bright red light coming from its throat. Transparent clear-coated black scales shot up to its mouth.

It let out a loud fiery roar towards Dametrix who ducked and cut its right leg. Fire shot towards the ceiling and the dragon roared loudly in anger, then fell on its right side, spraying fire everywhere. Dametrix jumped on its shoulder, but fell forward, sword first. He sliced the dragon's head off and fiery lava splashed everywhere out the neck. Dametrix then ran towards the front door.

"Knock-knock!" he yelled, then jumped high with both his feet, and kicked the door open, which sent King Everest flying backward.

Everest sat up facing the door and saw Dametrix proudly standing before him, holding the sword in his hand. "Name's Dametrix by the way," he said. "You're welcome. Have you got any other dragons?"

King Everest smiled. "You brave fool, that was a great performance," he said in amazement. As they walked with their horses down the mountain, Dametrix turned around and saw the sky clearing up, the snow sparkling like diamonds. "Looks like it's not dark anymore," he said.

King Everest turned around and smiled, then frowned when he heard a rumbling. They looked at each other. King Everest looked backwards and asked,"What is that?" Dametrix was already on his horse. He yelled, "I don't know, but I'm not sticking around to find out."

"Wait for me," King Everest screamed as he tried to get on his horse, looking back one final time and seeing a big wave of snow coming down from the top of the mountain. The king tried to catch up with Dametrix's horse.

"I told you so," Dametrix yelled back at him. As they got close to the bottom, the snow pushed into them, sending Dametrix flying into a tree. Minutes went by as Dametrix started looking for King Everest, yelling his name. The king yelled "I'm over here! My glove is stuck on this branch. Help me down, I'm scared of heights." Dametrix started laughing. "What? That makes no sense. You just came down from a mountain."

"That's different," Everest yelled. "With this if I fall, I will die. At least with the mountain if I fall, I'll roll down."

Dametrix shook his head and helped him down. "Wait, isn't that the glove you smacked me with?" King Everest said with excitement in his voice, "Thank you. Ye shall get rewarded for your bravery."

Dametrix looked confused. "For helping you down or killing the dragon?"

The king ignored his question. "I shall decree from this day on, ye mountain shall be named Dametrix!" With a sudden realization on his face, Dametrix said, "I think it will sound better with your name."

"Are thy sure? Ye kind man, there's no need to be noble. Thou hast already proven ye self. Mountain King Everest sounds – "

Dametrix cut him off. "OK, enough with the ye and thy, trust me it will stick. Just take out the king part."

"Ha, ye be a smart fool. My apologies, a great knight. May I see the sword? Get on a knee."

Dametrix gave him a weird look but did as he said. "I dub thee Dametrix as one of the great knights, just like Cousin Arthur." Getting up and recognizing the name, Dametrix mumbled, "Oh…"

"What?" King Everest replied

"Oh nothing, just thought about something."

The king said, "You almost got your butt kicked back there. Haha."

They got on their horses and rode off laughing. "You are a strange one," King Everest said.

With excitement in his voice, the king loudly spoke, "What land do ye, I mean, you come from. You're welcome to visit my land."

"I'm from New York, land of the brave crazy fools and dreams."

Everest smiled, "Explains a lot. Well, in my kingdom ye shall be welcome with open arms, food and women."

As they approached the kingdom, a large crowd spotted them and cheered. A beautiful woman approached Dametrix's horse, grabbed his hand and feet, opened her mouth and a buzzing sound came out.

He looked at her weird. "Oh no, no, no, no, nooo…"

He woke up to his alarm on the black dresser next to his bed, angrily looked at it, and slapped it.

DMT JOURNEYS

For the next few days, he progressed further, learning how to create weapons and fly, even dreaming about saving princesses. He sailed with sailors landing on a boat. Everyone cheered, "Arrr, ye air feet has come back to us and slain the Kraken. Three cheers for light feet!" Dametrix flew off the ship while waving goodbye to all the pirates, enjoying the wind through his hair and loving the feeling of being free.

The days of school were like a blur. All Dametrix could think about were his dreams. One of his teachers, Ms. Johnson, said to him one day, "Are you OK? You're always daydreaming, I don't know how you always get your homework done. You don't even look like you're paying attention most of the time." One day, as he was sitting at lunch by himself thinking, Stanly slammed his hand on the table.

Dametrix, surprised by it, screamed and the lunchroom got quiet as everyone looked at them. Stanly started laughing hysterically. Sam walked to the table and said, "Alright, go back to what you're doing." Surprisingly, everyone did. Stanly grinned, saying, "Yeah you better." "Shut up!" everyone screamed at him.

Sam tried to hide the fact that he wanted to laugh so hard. Dametrix didn't care, he was laughing. Martino walked to them with his lunch in hand. "Hey guys, how are you doing? Wow look, it's the infamous Dametrix!

Where have you been, Mr. Ghost? I haven't seen your presence for days."

"I've been here, you guys just been avoiding me." Everyone at the table stared at Dametrix with blank looks on their faces. Dametrix looked around. "What?"

"Well, let's spend some time after school since we're the ones avoiding you." Sam said.

"Don't waste your time," Stanly said. "All he does is make excuses."

Dametrix quickly said, "Yeah sounds like fun."

Stanly looked shocked. "What?" he mumbled while looking at Dametrix, who was giving him a smug look.

After enjoying his time with his friends catching up – Martino talking about how Sam got denied by Derica with everyone laughing, and going to the mall to eat, Dametrix couldn't wait to go home and sleep.

As he fell asleep, he landed in a grassy field. "Alright, let's have an adventure." He changed his clothes from black pants and a white shirt to all-white pants and shirt. He started off running, picking up more speed which left a trail of dust, then jumped off his feet to fly, creating a sonic boom, and leaving a contrail behind. He flew very quickly then slowed to enjoy the scenery and heard a faint sound. Lowering his altitude, the sound grew louder, but couldn't understand what it was.

All he saw was green cut grass below him. All around the barn, there appeared to be cut corn, but no house or people. There was a second red barn close by, which looked worn and its color was fading, but it had a freshly painted black door. A weird feeling went down his spine as he got closer to the back door. Not thinking anything of it, he opened the door and walked inside, cautiously looking around and seeing nothing but spider webs, broken wood, and hay everywhere. Getting a gut feeling that he should leave, he yelled, "Is anyone here? If not, I'm leaving!"

Every feeling in his body was saying "go back to that door." He turned towards it and started walking faster. Right before he touched the knob, he heard a scream, causing a hot feeling in his stomach and chills down his spine. The sound was echoing as Dametrix ran towards the scream located at the back of the barn, which seemed to be getting wider and bigger on the inside but didn't match how it appeared on the outside. Getting closer to the shouting, he could see dark movements and the closer he got, the more he saw what appeared to be two dark, muscular backs of men with long dirty hair wearing torn clothes.

He bravely smiled, "Leave her alone!" The men continued to face their backs towards him, bending over two human legs on the floor, which were kicking up and down trying to get up. Dametrix took a deep breath and shouted, "I said leave her alone! Do you not know who I am? I'm D!" Both men turned. One of the dark figures had a face and ears that were long like a goat's and he stood on hooves, roughly about five feet tall. The other dark figure had one pointy ear while the left ear had a piece of it missing. Its face was human, but very oily and covered with dirt and scratch marks. It also had short, sharp teeth like a piranha. Saliva dripped from the lips of both creatures onto the rocky ground.

They had dark yellow eyes like a cat's and were very focused on him. The dark figure with the goat face said menacingly, "What you say, human? Come closer, I can't hear you. After I finish this dinner, you're next for dessert."

Dametrix froze with fear, remembering that horrific night in bed when he was being choked. The human lookalike Dark Figure Two was holding the girl's left legs as she tried to crawl away while Dark Figure One with its goat hooves walked closer to him. "Come on, food," it said to him. Dametrix slowly backed away while the figure moved closer. He wanted to run away, but his feet now felt heavy.

A hot feeling from his gut gave him a burst of courage. "Enough of this," Dametrix said. "I'm not afraid of you." They jumped a little from being startled. Dametrix heard a voice saying, "Run you fool."

DMT JOURNEYS

"Who said that?" Dametrix swung his head left and right. "I'm not running, I can take them."

The voice replied, "No, you can't. If you die here, that's the end for you." The dark figures threw the girl towards the wall, knocking her out. Their yellow jagged teeth showed as they growled.

Dametrix turned around and ran towards the black door. The dark figures ran after him. He wasn't able to see the door anymore but was too afraid to attempt to fly, afraid of failing and getting captured. It seemed the faster he ran, the darker it got and longer the run and he couldn't see any way out. *Why am I even running? This is my dream, I can take them. This can't be real.*

All he could hear were little hooves clicking fast; then he felt a sharp pain in his back. He screamed loudly, turned his head, and saw dark, red, angry eyes and an open goatlike mouth with sharp teeth and saliva dripping. It got closer to him and was holding a piece of his bloody shirt and attempting to grab him again. "Why are you running? We just want to talk to you," the creature yelled at him.' Don't freaking run from me, you're only pissing me off more."

"Oh my God, I want to get out of here," Dametrix said to himself while running faster. "Oh God." Dametrix saw a door down the long hall and ran to it, hoping it was the black door, but as he got closer, he saw the door was white. Screaming "I don't care!" he charged at the door, burst through it, slammed it shut and dropped to the floor.

Bam! He looked up to see black tai chi shoes and socks, long black and tan silk suit pants, a long-sleeve tan suit shirt with a white stripe at the end of the sleeves and another white stripe going from the crease of the sleeves to the pants.

Dametrix tried to get up but fell back. He saw what appeared to be a young Chinese American with a black bowl-style haircut reaching just the top of his eyebrows, which were so perfectly and evenly cut. Strangely, this young-looking man had a long white beard, which didn't make sense. The half young-half old man asked bewildered, "Who are you? How did you get here?" Dametrix, with a happy look on his sweaty face and trying to catch his breath, smiled and said, "Aw man, thank you, old man for saving me." The man, still in a fighting stance, with his right leg stretched a little forward and his left leg bent behind him, tried to get a bit closer. His right and left arms formed acute angles and his hands were in fists. "Answer me or I will kill you."

Dametrix, with an angry look on his face, asked him, "Weren't you the voice that told me to run? Now, what the hell is it with this damn dream and everything trying to kill me?!"

The old man got up in a straight posture. "What did you say, kid?"

"Yeah, this damn dream sucks! I don't usually tell my dreams this is a dream, but yeah, sorry old man, you are not real. Out of all my dreams getting chased by those things, this is the weirdest one – besides the dream I had when that thing that   tried to choke me in my bed, which I still think happened for real."

The old man reached out his arm and Dametrix flinched before seeing that it wasn't a fist but an open hand. "People call me Jet, but you can call me Bruce Chan.

What's yours?"

Dametrix hesitated then grabbed Bruce's hand and got up. "I'm Dametrix."

Bruce smiled at the kid before him. "So you think this is a dream huh? I'm sorry to break it to you kid, it's not. Those things that were chasing you were probably demons."

"I don't believe you. That's a lie, who's their boss, the boogeyman?"

"Believe it or not, but the scratches on your back say otherwise, kid. I don't normally do this. You seem like an impertinent kid, so if you want, I can teach you how to defend yourself."

"You're a funny old man," Dametrix said and laughed. "Thanks, but no thanks. I can defend myself. Those stupid things just caught me by surprise. I won't be scared anymore."

"You think so? OK kid, why don't you show me these skills of yours. Try to land one punch on me if you can."

"I don't want to hurt you, old man."

"Trust me you won't, kid." Bruce put out his right hand, giving Dametrix a come-on gesture. Dametrix looked at Bruce standing there with a relaxed look on his face. It made him kind of worried as to why this old man looked so calm and confident as if he would win. Then, as if he read his thoughts, Bruce said, "As you age, you grow wiser. You call me an old man as if it's supposed to be an insult, kid."

Dametrix screamed, "Alright, you asked for it!" and charged at Bruce, afraid to hit him hard. He threw a light punch with his left arm, but as the hand hit Bruce's face the weirdest thing happened that just shocked him. Bruce disappeared. Dametrix looked around, confused, until he felt a tap on his right shoulder.

"Are you going to show me these skills or just stare at the vast emptiness of my world?" Startled by what Bruce just said, Dametrix jumped. "How the hell did you do that, old man?" Bruce reappeared in front of his face, smiled, and punched him, sending him flying and rolling backward. He got up slowly, "Ow… OK, that's it old man, you're starting to piss me off."

Bruce said calmly, "You have to think before you act, then let your body do the rest. Let your emotions be the wind that pushes your boat, but don't let it control you, for you should always be the captain steering your ship."

"No, don't start with the old-man-fortune-cookie saying. What the hell does that even mean? What's next, you going to tell me wax on and off? No thanks, Splinter."

Every attempt Dametrix made to land an attack failed, and always ended with Bruce sending him flying backwards. As Dametrix got up from the ground, crumbled rocks falling off him, he'd look at Bruce standing there calmly, with both arms behind his back.

"Are you going to hit me already like you said or just stare at me?" He stood with an angry expression on his face. His sclera had been dark red, but was turning into a black color the more he got mad. His iris turned into a bright red as he charged towards Bruce. With his eyes now all black, leaving a little red circle of his iris showing.

For Dametrix, everything moved slowly. He threw a punch with his right arm, but Bruce blocked it with his left arm. Doing so, he noticed Dametrix's eyes with a surprising look on his face. Dametrix ducked, faking as if he was going to side sweep Bruce's feet. Bruce jumped, but Dametrix quickly grabbed Bruce's leg with his left arm and slammed him down. Bruce kicked Dametrix off him and back-flipped on the floor.

He saw Dametrix already charging at him, tackled him to the floor, and stood over him. "I finally got you, old man," Dametrix said with an insidious stare. Bruce swept his feet as Dametrix fell to the floor and got up, throwing a punch with his right arm and creating a cloud of smoke. As it cleared, Dametrix was kneeling on a crater underneath his feet and looking at Bruce with a sinister smile. He blocked the next punch.

Bruce pulled his arm back. "Alright, that's enough," he said, backing away from Dametrix.

Dametrix laughed maniacally while getting up. "What's wrong, old man?" he taunted. "Now that I'm taking you seriously, you already   quitting   ?"

He shook his head. "No, I just seen   enough kid. Now submit."

Dametrix looked at Bruce, showing what appeared to be sharp teeth, and charged at him again. "I don't know how to," he shouted.

"You have heart, kid." Bruce disappeared and reappeared, ducked right next to Dametrix, and punched him in his stomach. Dametrix's eyes turned back to normal while saliva spilled from his mouth. He fell to his knees, holding his stomach. "OK fine, I'll let you win this time." he said as he passed out.

4   KNOWING IS LEARNING

*M*oments later, Dametrix looked up, seeing a hand, reached out and grabbed it. "I thought I lost you there stranger! I'm Dutch Dametrix, sensei."

With excitement, Dametrix said, as he was getting up, "Are you going to teach me how to do the cool things you can do like disappearing and reappearing? How did you get so fast?"

"OK, one step at a time, kid. You must learn before you know. Listen up, I don't know how you got here, but only a few can open a doorway to my realm and you don't look like any of them."

"Who is *them*? Why didn't you just say that before you attacked me?"

With an annoyed look, Bruce said, "I did not attack you, "I had to be sure."

"So what the hell is this place? Looks like a big ass empty store with no roof or wall."

"You can't just expect someone to tell the truth all the time, sometimes you have to let them show you without asking for it. It's a lot more reassuring than trying to guess if they are lying. Moving on, there are three planes or dimensions, symbolically speaking. I'm sure you are familiar with the humans who have given them many different names.

"There's the one you call heaven, purgatory in the middle, and at the bottom you have hell. Within each dimension, you have about two doors that are known. One door in every plane is the one that leads to the human world. You heard about it when someone who claims they saw a bright light. That's the first door. Or they have seen red and heard screaming going to the place you call hell. The other doors are back ways. Most demons or other beings use it to get to your side since they can't use the first door unless opened by a human that's deceased. Certain doors are easier to open than others. Those are the back doors for a small amount of time that can be opened by strong or sneaky entities. I'm sure you have heard of them. Someone claiming to see a ghost or monster. What you call ghosts are most likely demons or different beings that open a little door to your plane. Most of the time Their powers are so weakened from the whole process they can't do much damage to you. Maybe move things around, depending on how strong they were before coming to your plain.

"They can do damage to you if they find a way to get strong. Where you have people-possessing, that's them feeding on your aura, chi, soul, spiritual pressure, strength, you take your pick of the names. Look at it like this: your body is just a shell to contain your spirit through its passage. What I like to call lessons/tests so to speak. You might call it life. Some people learn of this and strengthen their spirit, which in return, also helps their bodies making it stronger and a better shell.

"Get your shell strong enough, you get what your kind call 'powers' or 'special abilities.' In truth, it is your spirit that has become so massive that it has more than enough to overfeed your other chakras. Your body feeds off your spirit and chakras, that is what makes your heart, mind, cells, etc. keep going. The major light bulbs

KNOWING IS LEARNING

in your body are your heart and mind, which cannot function alone. They all work together. Your spirit feeds your blood, which carries the energy all around your body feeding your organs similarly to the process of what oxygen does. If you can strengthen your spirit, your body will not be such a heavy burden on your spirit; hint: that is why you need to rest. You can become stronger, faster, better, live longer, and won't need to only depend on a proper diet. You won't get tired so easily and when your aura becomes really strong, you will be able to see it outside your body and see the universe for what it is.

"Are you aware of your weak eyesight? You can't even really see the other beings inhabiting your planet with you unless they make themselves known. You will also be able to open portals or doorways, whichever you prefer to call them. You need to have strong spiritual energy, that is the key. Let's number the levels, ten being the highest. Some doors require more energy than others or just something else. My door, you need a level nine and positive energy.

"Wait? For positive?"

Bruce replied, "Yes and negative energy. OK kid, I see I must go basic with you. How did you even end up here and not know anything about this? There is positive and negative energy. I am sure there's some people or situations where you felt bad energy from someone or

DMT JOURNEYS

104

something. That's someone leaving their imprints on it or their mark. An energy or aura is kinda like water. Do you know what water or aura is?"

"OK, old man, I'm not that dumb. Just keep talking about your heeby-jeeby stuff." Ow, why you smack me for? I said I was listening. Have you ever had someone sit on something for a long time or been somewhere and, when they leave, there's some sort of aroma?"

Dametrix replied, "Or made it hot and smelly? That's Stanly."

"Yes, kid, It's similar to that on the seat or room."

"Yeah, it's called a fart, ha ha ha. *Ow*."

"Energy can be compared to smells just as a dog or shark can smell something from a far distance. Each animal has its own specialty in a different environment and different explanation for it. You can also sense someone's energy echoing from far away, especially if it's strong enough in this ocean universe. Those are the things you will be learning and if you pay attention, you might be able to even pick up someone's energy and absorb it, learning all you can about that person. Only rare level tens can do that. Energy is all around you, it's what makes everything go and move. If you can master energy, learn to work with it, and make it work for you, and you with it, you can be incredibly powerful. However, there's a lock on every energy. Knowing how to unlock them and control it is the sign of a true master.

DMT JOURNEYS

"Some are easy to break. If you want, you could control the elements; it's the easiest to learn and also the hardest. Being able to work with water, earth, fire, air… there are legends turned to stories of great people being able to do these things. You can be great like them or even greater if you work hard and put your mind to it."

"Yeah, yeah Dad, I'll pass. I just want to know how to kick those things' butts. Why just know the basics when you can learn, be so powerful?" He opened his hand and he felt static. A white ball of fire appeared from his hand.

"You won't even have to kick their butts. They will just know you're nothing to be messed with."

Dametrix looked at him with an apathetic look on his face. "Yeah, no, that sounds like too much work. I can do like the cool people in the cartoons and become one with those demons and be strong that way." Bruce hit him again.

"Ow, what I do now?"

"Demons are not your friends, that's the dumbest thing I've ever heard. You humans have a real misconception about demons. Who do you think are telling you all those lies?"

"Um…for your info, old man, the people that make the cartoons—"

Bruce cut him off, raising his voice louder. "Yeah, people that work for the demons tell you that."

Dametrix got up. "That's not true! I don't believe it or this demon thing."

"No kid, it is not that you don't believe, 'cause you do. It's that you don't want to believe. Did you not just hear what I said? This isn't a joke kid; demons despise everything about you and would do anything that it takes to make sure you are in pain and suffering like they do.

"I've watched them kill countless things. Men, women, kids, and not care about anything but themselves." Dametrix sat back down looking at the floor as Bruce walked around him. "It is that selfishness idiotic thinking that leads you, humans, to become demon puppets," Bruce said. "Letting the darkness inside take over. The desires of evil nature. Greed, lust, anger, self-righteousness. Instead of dealing and facing the truth or your problems and dealing with them, you run or find an easier way."

He stood behind Dametrix and rubbed his beard with one hand while the other one was behind his back. "Now let's begin on your training."

Dametrix looked up excitedly. "Hell yeah!" He was met with an angry stare from Bruce.

"Do not say that," he shouted. "What, hell yeah." Dametrix laughed. "It's just words, remember old man? Sticks and stones."

Bruce looked at him with a calm yet angry frown on his face then stopped, slowly walking around him and, with his right hand, grabbed the back of Dametrix's shirt. A dark round hole appeared the moment Bruce lifted his left hand. He threw Dametrix into the hole.

The next moment, he landed on his stomach, his hands and body touching the floor. As he was lying on the rocky floor, he felt an excruciatingly hot feeling. He tried to get up, but it was so hard with every effort the weight of gravity pushed down more on him. He just found himself lying down again, feeling helpless. He was barely able to breathe, taking short breaths and gasping for what little hot, dry air there was. He kept blinking non-stop and his eyes quickly dried out. Everything hurt. Just looking around hurt   . There was darkness and a bright red light from a far distance. There were screams that at first sounded like they came from the light but then he realized they came from all around him.

He wanted to cry but was unable to since the tears evaporated as they left his tear ducts, leaving salty, dry residue underneath his eyes. The same happened to his sweat, leaving a salt trail. His lips were chapped, sunburned, and blistering from exposure to the atmosphere. He could smell the overwhelming scent of burning ash, plus just about anything you could think of: paper, clothes, garbage, meat, smog high in the air with ash falling from the sky. The crackling sound of someone walking on rocks grew closer and closer.

DMT JOURNEYS

The walk was going the same rhythm as his heart. Dametrix panicked, trying not to make any noise, and trying to take fewer breaths. Feeling light-headed and frustrated, he hated himself. *I had the great moment of learning to defend myself and get stronger. I let it go by being stupid. That damn Bruce Chan, it's his fault, I hate him. Is it my fault? No, it's his!* He bickered with himself, back and forth. *I would never be here. I should have never played with this.*

"You smell that?" the voice asked. "It smells good…" The sounds got louder, faster, closer.

His heart was now racing, as glowing floating eyes approached him.

"Please save me G−"

"Look at what I found!"

His heart dropped. He saw a pig foot with blisters and cuts on them. Looking up, he saw more nasty, hairy legs with boils, ripped pants, an overweight body, and a shirt that appeared to be made from skins. There was a face reassembling a pig's with sharp pointy teeth, red eyes. The creature held a big, rusted, broken fork. *I see now why demons have red eyes. Is this a demon? Am I going to die?*

Another footstep followed after the first one and that voice cried out, "This one is mine, I'm hungry!" The human face showed up out of the dark distance. Its skin was peeling, there were cuts on its face and body, skinny arms and legs, and its ribs were showing. It had what appeared to be a square mustache. "I'm hungry too, master," said the one with the square mustache. They both laughed. A light appeared and they froze in fear.

A voice said, "Don't worry about me."

Dametrix's heart jumped with joy, and a smile slowly appeared until he heard Bruce. "He's all yours. He said he wanted to be friends with demons. Well, now is your chance!"

They began to smile and laugh, keeping a distance at the same time trying to grab Dametrix on the ground with the fork, scratching his arm and face while reaching with long bony fingers with chipped nails that scratched him more.

"Yeah, come on boy. Come play with us, we'll have fun," the other one said, licking its lips as saliva dripped on the ground. "Well go ahead, isn't this what you wanted?"

"Sor – *ry*..." Bruce took a step forward and they looked at him with anger. He grabbed Dametrix and they went through the portal as the demons rushed forward to grab them. The portal closed and Dametrix tried to get up from the floor, but fell to his knees. Steam rose off his body, and tears were streaming from his eyes. He promised to himself he would never let anyone make a fool out of him or be weak again.

Bruce looked at him. "You ready to be serious now, boy?"

"Yes sensei," Dametrix replied.

Bruce, putting his hand inside his sleeves, said, "First thing: you have to meditate in order to build up your spirit and on your side of the plane, you have to work out until I tell you to stop. Then, when you are ready, I will train you to fight. When you go back to your world, rehearse the same things you learn so you develop muscle memory. Therefore, your subconscious will be able to react on its own, sharpening your instincts."

Dametrix replied, his voice breaking and sounding dry, "What if I train here and meditate out there?"

Bruce replied, "No, here is where the spiritual presence is stronger and not tainted, which can easily help strengthen yours. You're not clouded by distractions like out there; you can better your mind. Out there, you can strengthen your physical training. Make sure you only focus on your task. I repeat, all you have to do is workout – one hundred push-ups and sit-ups, then run one mile. I'm sure you would not meditate properly on your own or even do it at all because you might think it's boring."

Dametrix smiled, "Fine. How will I find this place you said it can't be easily found?"

"Don't worry kid, I'll find you. Now wake up!"

A loud buzz rang and he opened his eyes, looked at the clock and then accidentally pushed it on the floor. "Ow!" He quickly got up, checked his arms and legs and ran to the bathroom to study his back. There were no scratches, no marks. Nothing. He walked to the bus stop and started to question whether it was all real.

A voice rang out. "Hey, hurry up! We have a surprise for you! Guess who came back from boot camp?"

Sam stood tall, wearing a camouflage shirt and pants with black boots and a big smile on his face. He yelled to Dametrix and Dametrix ran toward him, surprised."Whoa, look at you. You changed, Sam."

"Me? Look at you, you changed yourself, D! Dametrix replied with a surprised look on his face. I didn't even know you left for boot camp. How could you? I hear you have been ignoring the group, walking to school by yourself, leaving Stanly with Martino alone. You know he's a princess, he can't be left alone. He gets into trouble, especially with that big mouth of his, dragging poor Martino with him."

They all started laughing. "I'm just messing with you!" Stanly's laugh was not sincere. "Ha, yeah, we miss you man. Apparently, it's not a full boot camp. It was pre-boot camp, whatever that means. My parents made me do this program."

Martino smiled, "Yeah, we miss you loser."

Sam opened his arms. "Come here man," and he hugged both Martino and Dametrix,

"I miss you too buddy," said Dametrix, replying to Martino. What have you been up to?" As the bus approached, Martino talked about how he stayed after school because he didn't want to be left alone with Stanly since he was always trying to do something bad. He enjoyed the fun but didn't like the repercussions. As they climbed onto the bus, everyone greeted Sam with welcome praise, especially the girls. He was so cool; it was like the other guys didn't even exist.

Everyone else looked at Dametrix as if he was a stranger they hadn't seen before or someone who had been gone a long time. Martino sat next to Dametrix while Stanly, as always, sat next to Sam. "Hey D, come sit next to me so I can talk to you about something." Stanly looked excited like he could not wait to hear, so he moved to the side, trying to make space. "Can I talk to him alone, Stanly? I'll tell you guys later." He got up with a snobby look on his face and slowly smiled the closer he got to Martino.

"Oh no," Martino groaned. "Oh, come on buddy, it won't be that bad. I have a plan I've been meaning to talk to you about, like old times, but since you started staying after class, I see less of you."

Dametrix laughed and sat. "Poor Martino! What did you want to talk about, bud?"

"Before we start . . ." He plucked a strand of hair from Dametrix's head. "Do you have a white strand of hair in front of your head?"

Dametrix grabbed his hair in surprise. "What, really?! Where?" He studied the strand of white hair. "Is that why everyone has been looking at me weird?"

"It's probably that and the fact you're always hiding from people, staying by yourself, or locking yourself up in your room. What the hell is up with that, are you OK?"

Dametrix looked around the bus on the word "hell." "Hey, no, It's not a good word to use. Be careful. They might be all around us."

"Um...OK, that was creepy man, what are you talking about?"

"Nothing, forget it."

"No, tell me, I want to know. Do you know about the kids that have been disappearing around us?"

Confused, Dametrix said, "Um, no. I didn't know kids were disappearing."

"No surprise there. Again, it's 'cause you've barely been around anyone. I was thinking you saw something weird and it scared you so maybe that's why your hair is white, you know, like in the cartoons." Martino laughed. Dametrix smirked, "Ha, not funny. That was a Stanly move with that lame joke."

"Yeah, I know, I seriously think it has something to do with that creepy studio place."

"Wait, you talking about the other house where they make music?"

"I think that's just one of them," Sam said. "There's a place close to it I want to check it out with you one day. I would ask the others, but Martino is too young, so that would scare him, and Stanly, well, he's Stanly. He might make a joke out of it or just be himself and somehow get in trouble."

Dametrix looked at him. "Oh yeah, 'cause sneaking into a place, that's not bad or won't get you in trouble, right, Sam."

"Do you hear yourself? Trust me, you don't need Stanly for this one to get in trouble."

"You just got back from boot camp. Why don't you just relax and enjoy your last year of school?"

"It's almost over? Wow, I can't believe school is almost over. It was just like yesterday, the first day of school I was telling you guys about my dream and you all laughed."

"Come on man, it will be like old times. Wait, are you trying to hold a grudge? I didn't laugh. Remember we used to go on adventures and do fun things together when Stan used to disappear with Martino trying to rob people? Besides, I'm going to college soon.

"Yeah, because he was mad, saying you stole me away from him. Man, it must suck huh? College and scholarship for football, you poor guy; being the coolest guy ever, that must suck too."

"Haha OK, sarcasm. I get it. Trust me, being popular isn't all that great sometimes. If you let it get to you, it will get you in trouble; that's why I like being with you guys, you just like me for me. Well, maybe not Stanly. I think he likes telling everyone that we're friends because of my popularity. Martino, a freshman hanging out with us, he's just happy to have friends. He's a cool little kid, smart but impressionable.

"You my best pal, homie, home skillet, buddy, I can go on for days we've known each other for years."

"No, you have been around me for years we always go to the same school, but you always had a group of people around you. The only reason you noticed me was because of Derica. You saw her talk to me, assumed we were friends and asked me about her; you didn't even care to ask if she was my girlfriend."

Sam laughed in response, "Ha, ha, yeah, good times. Well I figured she wouldn't because she was way too hot, um, I mean, I figured she would just be your best friend."

"Yeah, you can say it, she's too hot to be with us 'cause she turned you down. Haha."

"Wait, no she didn't. Sam the man never gets rejected, she was just being too difficult."

"Don't even matter, you immediately lost interest in her when you saw her friend, Katy, from Baton Rouge, Louisiana."

"Ah, Miss Ortiz, she was so hot and had a cute little voice. I wonder what happened to her."

"You left her for Makayla from Mississippi. You know, the black and Asian one."

"Oh, come on, a great awesome mix like that, you wouldn't try to talk to her because she was super hot."

"Yeah, you left her for Gabrielle, then there was Esther who moved to Orlando and was Guyanese, then there was the white and Spanish girl from Orlando and moved to Georgia who you met online."

"OK, OK, OK, fine I get it! And for the record, I liked those girls, and they could have been my wife, but they messed it up."

"Right, did they?"

Sam cut him off. "So buddy, are you going to come join me, please? I don't think you're a loser, by the way, if you just have more confidence in yourself and talk to people more, you can be cool too. That's where it starts."

Dametrix grunted. "Thanks for the lesson. You should write a book cool guy. Call it 'Sam's Journeys.' Really, no. Stop with the puppy dog eyes, you are not even doing it right and you are way too big 'n tall to be doing that look."

"Fine I'll go with you. Just let me know when you want to go."

Sam cheered. "Yeah, thank you, man, hell yeah!"

5   THOU SHALT NOT

*L*ater that night while trying to sleep, a door appeared in front of Dametrix. He opened it to see Bruce
standing before him, almost like he was waiting for him.
Stepping through the white door, his clothes changed
into a karate outfit with a yellow belt around his waist.
Bruce smiled, "Have you been practicing kid?"

"Uh...yeah—" Bruce hit him. "Ow! What was that for?"

"Do not get distracted!"

Dametrix stared at Bruce. "OK, fine old man. I was hanging out with my friends. You know, the thing I can't do ever since I've been trying to do this dumb sleep thing. I'm now realizing how much of my life I'm missing out of. It's been six months, if not more time, I've put into this, missing out on my friends. I'm tired of this. Maybe it was a bad dream like Stanly said. This is probably a bad dream too, you telling me to work out so I can think it's real 'and your help is why my body is changing, instead of the obvious. It's just from working out. All your aura crap isn't real. Me over thinking is the cause of all these nightmares.

"Well… is that what you think?" Bruce hit him again. "Ow, stop hitting me!"

"If this isn't real, why say 'ow'," Bruce retorted. "Why keep having the same dream and feel it like it's real? Your physical body isn't affected because you're in your soul form right now. It replenishes when you give your body a chance to rest."

Dametrix rolled his eyes. "Yeah, yeah, yeah, I heard it before. You guys say the same thing. Wait, ya took that from a movie, didn't you? Next, you're going to want me to take some colored pills, huh old man? Do I need to watch my back?"

Bruce hit him again. "Owww."

"Take this seriously or do you need to visit your other friends again? They can show you the easy way."

He then lifted his left hand in the same manner as last time, opening his palm and showing all five fingers towards Dametrix. Dametrix quickly sat on the floor, quietly, with his eyes closed, peeking out his left eye. His legs were crossed like a pretzel. Bruce turned around. "Focus! Listen kid, every choice has its consequences and sometimes it's greater than you want it to be. Other times, you don't even notice you're paying. Train hard so you can protect yourself and your friends and family."

"Don't worry about me, old man. I have no family, just me and my grandma." Bruce stroked his long beard, circling Dametrix. "Interestingly, you have your friends. I'm sure you care for them like your family. Be patient and good comes to those who work hard."

"Where did you steal that from, a fortune cookie?" Bruce smacked his head. "Ow…"

As time progressed, so did Dametrix, strictly following the directions assigned to him because he was afraid of what that calm old man had up his sleeves. Surprisingly, he started enjoying the workouts. He did hundred pushups a day, swam laps, ran for a mile, and ate protein and plantbased foods. Since he was loving it so much, he sometimes missed days of school and went to train away from distractions and his grandma. His dedication was growing more with every result. He didn't know how it happened but every time he slept, he would just see a door and walk through it wearing the same karate outfit. The only thing that changed was the color of the belt around his waist, nothing else. He always ended up in that empty, endless warehouse where Bruce Chan was waiting for him.

Bruce looked at him angrily. "Why aren't you progressing as you should be? This is taking too long."

A look of confusion appeared on Dametrix's face as he yelled, "What, are you serious? I've done everything you asked me to do and more."

Bruce raised his right hand. "Quiet, this is your last chance. Meditate. I have to think about what I will do with you." In a half-lotus position, Dametrix closed his eyes, hearing mumbling. He focused and listened and felt a smooth, yet calm feeling pass from his body to his ear.

As he focused, words went from being muffled to becoming abundantly clear. "I have to find something or that's it for the kid. That's it, Bruce."

Bruce noticed Dametrix peeking at him and raised his hand. "I know what to do," he said to himself. Bruce appeared next to Dametrix. "There you go, kid, now you're ready."

Confused, Dametrix opened his eyes. He was over the ground while a white ball of black static and energy crackled around him. He tried to uncross his legs, but then realized he was floating, and landed on his feet. He jumped up with joy.

Bruce, with a smile on his face for once, said, "I can teach you the time step."

Dametrix was miffed. "What you called the disappearing trick." He smiled and started dancing while running around Bruce, repeatedly yelling, "Yes! My favorite one!"

"OK settle down," Bruce said. "Remember that time is always moving; if you can charge your energy to the point where you push yourself to move so fast that the naked eye can't keep up, you would look like you disappeared in the blink of an eye."

Dametrix looked at him, seemingly confused and dissatisfied. "Why call it a time step if it has nothing to do with time? You're just going fast!"

"Not bad. You're close but not there yet. It's a good start. You're paying attention but don't be so quick to jump into stuff. You need to think before you act because once you master it, you could possibly move through time. Time is already written. That's how people can see into the future and so on. They just see into the written or future that already happened."

"Oh, OK."

"So let's say there's a wall stretched far that has every event that's happened and is going to happen written on it and those who can see into the future can just move their minds from one spot to another.

"They exist in one point in time on the wall and then move their mind forward or backward down the wall, seeing the future or past. That means that time is always moving at one pace. Charging your chi could cut through space a little bit, making everything around you appear to be moving slowly, and to them, you would just be moving faster. You can break the hold it has on you. By using your chi as a shield, it would protect you from its effects. I believe the closest thing to humans understanding this is in what they call 'time dilation'.

"Remember kid, everything comes with a consequence. You're moving fast when you're using your abilities. Remember there are strong beings out there that can sense you just as you can sense them, waiting for a smaller fish. Always train if you can do better to be better. There's always someone on top."

"What kind advice is that?" Dametrix replied, confused. "That was really depressing." His words were met with silence. Bruce stared at him while stroking his beard. After looking at Dametrix for some time, he said, "Impatience will cause you pain. While there are always going to be greater challenges. That is why you should never forget your training. Always strive to be better than you were yesterday.

DMT JOURNEYS

"The mind and spirit learn to control and push because it has no limit of how strong it can get. You might even telepathically control what's around you when you get to a master state. You can have enough qi to create things and control them too. That's how you can gain greater abilities like open portals.

"When your qi is so strong, you think of a place, channel your ki precisely, and burst through reality and go where you want. That is at a master level few can reach. I believe only five beings can do that and only a couple can come through my reality because I exist in a plane outside of yours—"

"Is that why you attack me?" Dametrix interrupted Bruce. "So, what exactly are you, like an alien using a human body? Are you probing me, and this is just an illusion? You look like a person like I've seen you before, yet you keep separating yourself, calling us humans."

Bruce eyed him and smiled. "Yes, I once was a human. Little, stubborn, and cocky. I am beyond that now, I had a lot of time to think and train to find my peace. I try to keep this look for I feel that's how I would look if I didn't die ahead of my time."

"Wow, what the−?"

Bruce gave him a scary look and he quickly looked down. "Enough questions. Show me you can do it and if you do, I'll offer you a bonus reward."

"Yeah, let's do it!" Dametrix exclaimed, jumping on his tip toe back and forth. "You ready to have your mind blown, sensei?"

"The lips can always bring you somewhere that you can't handle. Make sure the mind is guiding it, not the heart."

Dametrix rolled his eyes. "Yeah, yeah, yeah, you and your damn riddles. I feel like you have a bag of fortune cookies hiding somewhere." Dametrix balled up his fist and looked up at the white void of emptiness.

Bruce put one hand behind his back and moved the other one forward as Dametrix started to pose and yell in a squat. "What are you doing, kid?" he asked. "Why are you yelling?"

"I don't know, I saw it in a cartoon, I'm powering up," Dametrix replied.

Bruce reappeared behind him and smacked his head. "Ow."

"No yelling," Bruce retorted. "It's not the time for that, now focus and get in your stance."

"What's the point of a stance? I always saw them in the movies and cartoons." Bruce walked away from him with his hands behind his back as he said, "Fighting is a strategic art. Your stance is your brush. The way you fight is your color. Just like if you're going to draw the picture, you need to think about what you're going to draw, planning what you need to do to get to your goal."

Despite that Bruce was walking away from him, Dametrix could still hear him clearly as if he were right next to him. Now there was about ten feet of distance between them both. Bruce stopped. "Now try to get where I'm at. Picture yourself running fast and really wanting to be here. Use that feeling you did when you were trying to listen to what I was saying."

"Hold on old man, you knew about that?"

With a smile, Bruce explained, "It was my plan all along, now focus."

After numerous tries, he failed and failed, pushing himself backwards and forward. Most of the time, he ended up landing face first. Bruce raised one eyebrow. "OK, let's try something else. See if you can catch me as I time step away from you. Try to use your mind more than your legs."

Bruce ran with Dametrix running faster than faster, one of his arms out, trying to touch Bruce. It always seemed he was inches away. "You're not doing it right, kid. I'm not asking you to run faster with your legs. Come on, stop trying to catch me, just catch me already! Catch me now before it's too late."

Bruce disappeared right in front of his eyes. Dametrix looked around and couldn't see Bruce anymore. He then looked behind him to see Bruce chasing him with a sword made of energy. He swung and cut Dametrix's back.

"What the hell is your problem, old man?" Dametrix yelled in pain. "Why did you do that?"

Bruce yelled, "What did you just say? I warned you…" He raised his arm. "That's it, back to the portal for you."

Several portals opened in front of Dametrix, who was trying to not get caught by Bruce or fall into the dark, round portals. He jumped out of the way, ran, and jumped up very high. "I'm sorry," he exclaimed.

Bruce touched his back. "Gotcha!" And just like that, Dametrix disappeared. He reappeared a foot away from Bruce and tripped, then rolled on the ground. He quickly got up and started to run before Bruce appeared in front of him. He screamed and disappeared away from Bruce.

"Look kid, you're doing it," Bruce said as he watched him.

Dametrix stopped as he heard that and saw Bruce, who was now far away from him. "Oh my gosh… yay, I did it!" he exclaimed excitedly. "Ha, can't touch this."

Bruce appeared in front of him. "Yes, I can," he replied as he disappeared. Dametrix appeared, away from Bruce.
"No you can't – na na na na na na na."

"Ha, good job Dutch."

"I can't believe you called me by my name," he laughed while loudly repeating, "Yes, yes, yes."

"As I promised, your reward is Seven, one of the most powerful weapons ever."

"Then why does it have such a dumb name?"

Bruce smacked his head. "Ow."

"Be respectful," Bruce said. "It once belonged to an enormously powerful being. You are going to need these glasses. As he said that while opening the palm of his right hand, a pair of glasses appeared. "I don't think you are able to see clearly; your eyes aren't strong enough. Now wake up!"

Dametrix woke up to the alarm sound again. "Ugh," he muttered. "I just need a couple more minutes." He looked over and saw the clock reading five am.

He looked again. It now read five-forty am. *Wait, what could this have happened? Oh my gosh, not again! Why didn't I just get up today? OK, I'm wearing shorts, socks, and sandals, I don't care what anyone says. Oh no, I hear the bus! Where's my bookbag and my black shirt?* He ran out the front door and saw the bus leaving.

"Oh no, not today!" He focused and ran right past the bus all the way to the next bus stop and straight into Derica. He quickly grabbed her before she could fall. She smells so nice like sweet flowers and so hot with her black shirt and nice blue shorts showing that thick –

"Hey."

"Oh, hey." She looked at him and smiled. "Thanks for catching me. You let me go now?" He let her go. "Sorry about that."

"Yes, I made it and didn't fully make a fool of myself!" he thought while walking to school. "Today might be a good day." He felt good about himself. Everyone was so jealous he got to touch Derica. Even Sam was a little jelly. Before long, I heard, "Hey loser, what you got for me today?" It was W.D. bullying someone, and again, no one was doing anything about it. He grabbed the freshman by the backpack. Dametrix grabbed his hand and replied, "He's got nothing for you today or ever. Leave him alone and give him a break. What if it was you being bullied or your family or friends?"

"Then I would have grown one and fought back. Now move and mind your own business, hero boy."

"Well, maybe since your face scares him and you smell, that's why he doesn't   want to fight you." Everyone stopped and gathered around them, saying, "Ohhh." With an angry smile, he replied "What, are you trying to be funny?''

"No, your face pretty much does it all by itself. I'm your bully now. Why don't you grow one – '' Before Dametrix could finish, W.D. threw a punch and he saw it as if it was in slow motion, then instinctively caught

W.D.'s fist while it was in motion. He moved the freshman out the way. W.D. ran up to his face.

Dametrix realized everyone was moving slowly again, then it went back to normal. He breathed heavily and as W.D. threw another punch, he pushed it away.

Why did I get out of breath? he thought. *Am I using a lot of energy to do that damn time step? How do I do it?* Time began to slow down again. *Wow, so this is real. I'm so confused, but I like it.* A little evil smile grew on his face. "Come on!"

OK, I can do this again, I have to concentrate like Bruce said. With time moving so slow, he punched W.D, sending him flying down the hallway. *OK, I think I'm done. That knocked the wind out of me.* He went up to the freshman "Alright kid. Are you OK?" With the biggest smile he'd ever seen, the kid said, "Wow! Thanks, man, I appreciate it."

The kids kept chanting "Fight, fight, fight!" while others said things like, "Damn, I didn't know he was so strong." Breathing hard, Dametrix said arrogantly, "Oh, it was nothing."

He walked up to W.D as he was on the floor. "How does it feel now that you're being bullied? And being someone's − " The bell rang before he could finish. All his friends grabbed him. "Come on, man, let's go." Kids passed over W.D on the floor as he was saying in embarrassment, "Don't you snitch too."

DMT JOURNEYS

While sitting at lunch, everyone was saying hi and girls were smiling at him. "Man, is this what it feels like to be the hero?" he wondered. He couldn't wait to go back home and sleep. *I think Bruce's teachings are working. Is this real?*

Oh my gosh, he thought as he laid in bed later that day.

The same door as always popped up and he yelled, "Old man!"

"Will you ever call me by my name?" Bruce replied grumpily.

"I do, old man, ha! But guess what, I defended a kid today at school and you were right about that energy. I time skipped, I think, and pushed him flying in the air."

Bruce replied, "You did what?! Don't ever use your power on people outside of here! That was dangerous, what if you killed him?"

"What? Why are you getting grumpy about it?" Dametrix replied, confused. "I helped someone out. So, what if I use my powers, I earned them! You're supposed to be proud... whatever, old man." He turned his back and started walking away.

"Hold on, kid, I'm not mad because you helped someone. That was a noble thing you did – just doing the right thing and being brave; you don't need powers to do them. That bully felt like you overpowered him. You never know what your actions can cause.

Humans do crazy things when they are desperate, feel powerless, or just do things out of jealousy. All I'm saying is be careful of your cause, you never know what the effect will be."

Dametrix turned around and smiled. "So, I was kinda right for once, ha, ha."

Bruce frowned. "You're not getting the point and I didn't fully say that."

"Yeah, whatever, yes you did, old man. I want to keep meditating to get stronger."

"I hope you're doing it for a good cause. Always remember to only use your powers when you have to and never kill because you don't know the effects of taking a life. Now, enough meditation. You have something to do, don't forget."

Bruce explained, "I will make a portal open for you at exactly midnight. Be there at that exact time. That's around the time doors between the planes are weak enough for me to do it. Be ready, I'll try to detect where you are as much as I can. Now hurry and go. Wait. Hold on."

"Oh come on, you told me to go, now you're saying stay? Make up your mind."

Bruce raised his arm and Dametrix ducked, raising up his hands to cover his head. Bruce tapped him on the head. "I am proud of you. Not many can do what you do. Never forget to always follow your instincts. Your mind is the leader, your heart is the map. Don't let the map tell you where to go; you make the path. Your instincts are your compass. Always use all three equally to find your way. Here comes the hard part: do not show your abilities to anyone. Do you hear me, Dutch? Not even your friends or family."

"It should be easy to remember since I have no family."

"That's not entirely true, you have me now," Bruce said with a smile on his face.

"Whoa! Was that a smile? Someone must be waking up on the right side of the bed. Do you even sleep? All I see a vast amount of emptiness. Wait, one more thing, how long is this going to take because I want to go out with my friends?" Bruce looked at him and placed his right hand on Dametrix's left shoulder. Dametrix's body began vibrating while Bruce yelled at him to wake up. "No, don't say what will happen. Once I go in the portal, then what do I do next? Ahhh!"

He woke up sweating, looked around the room, and got up to go to the bathroom. After taking a piss and going towards the sink to wash his hands,he looked up at the mirror. And screamed.

What the hell happened to my hair? It's even more white! It looks like someone just took a brush with white paint and ran a line from the front of my hair all the way to the back. Is it white in the back?

DMT JOURNEYS

He couldn't tell − maybe it was paint. Stanly said he had a plan for Martino. Maybe he came in here to dye his hair. He tried washing it but the white wouldn't come out. *Damn it Stanly. Wait till I see you. I'll make you pay always with your damn jokes.* Bruce's face just popped up in the mirror screaming, "What are you doing kid go outside now? So surprised falling backwards trying to grab the sink and fall on the floor.

"Was that Bruce I just saw? Oh man, I'm losing my mind. Let me put on some clothes." He walked outside, looking around at the darkness with one street lamp flickering. *What am I even doing outside? This isn't even real.*

"Yes it is, Dametrix."

"Who said that and how do you know my name? Stanly, come on, this isn't funny anymore. Come out." He looked left and right and saw nothing but houses in the dark.

"You're still in denial after all I've done for you. I was the one that saved you and told you to run."

This can't be real. He thought it was a dream.

"Wait, so you are not the old man, Bruce?"

"If I were you I would be wary of him. Not everything is what it seems. He was the one that trained me to help me get strong. Have you actually gotten any stronger? What new powers or tricks have you acquired?"

DMT JOURNEYS

135

"Um . . . I got faster and stronger."

The voice mockingly laughed. "That's due to meditating."

"Maybe it's your soul he's after."

"No, I don't believe it if he was trying to hurt me he would have done it," Dametrix said. "He hasn't."

"Probably cause you're being manipulated."

"There's another animal they do that to."

"Don't worry about it, turkey. Have you noticed any changes to your appearance?"

Dametrix scratched his head. "Yeah, my hair is turning white, but no, that's my friend that did that. It couldn't be him."

"Was there leftover residue of dye on your pillow?"

Dametrix shook his head while listening to the voice. Feeling uncomfortable and angry, Dametrix interrupted. "Well, he said he gave me glasses so I can see where the glasses are, OK? If I can trust you then why don't you show yourself? "Or teach me yourself?"

The voice replied gently, "You will meet me in due time. I don't want Bruce to detect I'm trying to help you, thus end up hurting you because of it. I will walk you through how to make your own glasses. You don't need his.

"Just take a deep breath, relax, place your hands on your chest, touch over your heart. Feel the beat of it. Picture your own designer sunglasses. Do you feel that hot feeling on your chest? Focus your energy now when you feel you have a grip on it. Pull the glasses out. Good, Dutch, you're doing it. Wait. What's that?"

A big smile stretched across Dametrix's face as his eyes brightened up. As the white light grew brighter and brighter.

The glasses had appeared in his hands. This is the portal like he said. Wow, so cool.

The voice shouted, "Wait, no, fool, I don't think it's a great idea." The portal appeared like a round circle of white light.

Dametrix placed his finger on it. It felt warm and there was a breeze coming from it.

Disregarding the warning he placed his hand inside the portal. It quickly pulled his hand inside like a vacuum. He tried to pull his hand out but pulled the rest of his body in. The bright light just flashed in his face as if someone turned on the lights. His eyes hurt from being in that dark alley. He felt for the glasses in his hand and quickly put them on. A huge figure of a man stood before him. He screamed and fell backwards.

The shape didn't move. Sizing up the figure, he saw it was a big statue of what might be a man wearing a medieval helmet that he had only seen in video games. Standing on a plinth. Around the lower part of the face, covering the nose all the way down to the neck were different designs, like what were painted on ninjas. Its hair grew underneath and out the back of the helmet. The statue wore armor covering its whole body, with spikes coming from the arms and shoulders. Each corner of the room had the same statue, only each one had a different pose. Trying to stand on the slippery floor, Dametrix almost slipped to break his fall. He grabbed the statue with his left hand and touched the white wall with his right. Dust blew away. Writing appeared.

Amazed, he waved his hand – more and more writing appeared along with pictures. The pictures lined up, side by side, on the walls. In one picture the statue seemed to be fighting a great big beast with horns. In another picture the statue stood next to the pyramids. In another, it was next to a boat, then next to a man close to a mountain and surrounded by people.

There were also writings on the plinth, explaining the statues on each of the four corners of the room. Each held two different objects: a sword and a gun. Dametrix walked towards the middle of the room to get a view of the entire room. A cracking followed by scraping sound, like rocks rubbing on each other, opened up the marble floor. A gold stone pillar lifted up from the opening.

A square glass case appeared on top of the gold stone. He got closer and a gun appeared – a Magnum fifty-caliber Desert Eagle. A large number "seven" took up most of the space on the grip. Placing his hands on the glass, he saw bright yellow words on the glass that read: "Evil will be cast out." Then the glass disappeared. Around the case were glowing words that said: "D. One seven allowed."

A faint voice echoed in pain. The number seven began to glow. So did the gun. A flash was followed by an explosion that pushed Dametrix out of the portal back to the dark street where he once was. Brushing himself off he heard the voice say, "I told you no. He sent you to retrieve a weapon for him, maybe to help him get stronger so he can finish you off.

"Trust me Dametrix I have a better one that's stronger."

A portal opened like a mouth and a cold breeze sent shivers along his spine. He stopped inside the doorway and heard the voice again. A necklace appeared around his neck with a round glass medallion and a compass inside to help him find his way, to guide him where the energy of that object or place was. The voice exclaimed, "Consider it a gift!"

Dametrix looked around. "Yeah, I think I'm going to need it."

It was a terrible place. Dry, dead trees were everywhere. There was light enough to see a little bit but not far. Bones hung off trees and on the ground were glowing dots of light, like eyes or fireflies. Movement came from the trees and it sounded like branches breaking. It was hard to make out what was going on because of the thick fog.

DMT JOURNEYS

Dametrix started to walk slowly, watching his steps. He wanted to move faster but it felt like if he did it would make more noise. Whispers rose in the air – "What are you doing here? Oh, fresh meat, how did you get here?" As he walked in the very dim forest filled with the heavy odor of death, decay, dirt, it seemed his body was glowing.

"The weapon you are looking for is also a gun but called Six."

With a blank stare on his face, Dametrix replied, "Really? You people don't put much into naming, huh? Surprised you didn't just call it the gun or the weapon. Ha ha ha..."

The voice laughed. "That's good, keep up that sense of humor. I, too, have one." Just like that it got silent.

Dametrix had been walking and closed in on a big tree.

"Um... how do I find this gun? How long do I have to keep walking in this dark forest? All this keeps doing is pointing forward." Suddenly all the background noise stopped – there was no more whispering or tree branches breaking. The fog appeared to clear out. A loud deep voice seemed to shake the ground with its words. "Begone from this place you filthy thing!"

"Don't you dare come any closer or I'll make you pay!" Dametrix said.

"Who said that?" He approached a giant oak tree with a hole in the middle of it. "OK voice, are you trying to be funny?" The loud echoing voice screamed out again: "Come any closer and I will kill you."

Not watching where he was going, Dametrix bumped into the giant oak tree. Its branches appeared to be arms with skinny, bony fingers. The large hole in the middle looked like a big mouth. Dametrix took a deep breath and screamed, "I'm tired of being afraid of these damn dreams. I'm in control." A red glow started to illuminate from the hole in the tree. He leaned a little bit closer to see what it was. Then closer, closer, closer and he saw the shape of a gun similar to the one he had seen before.

This one had a large number six engraved into it and appeared to be glowing dark red. Mesmerized from just looking at the gun he couldn't take his eyes off it. *Wow, that is the coolest thing I've ever seen.* He heard a loud noise and to his right noticed a very pale male figure with ripped clothes and scratches everywhere, from its face down to his long nails feet. It called him "Food."

Reaching out its hands towards Dametrix, it said, "Give me that gun fool and I won't hurt you."

His surprise turning to anger, Dametrix said, "Besides the fact you look like Freddy with long nails, what killed it for me is that you called me food. Makes it really hard to trust what you say."

The man charged at him with an angry look. Dametrix quickly reached and grabbed the gun and pointed it at the man. The gun turned into a big eight-legged spider with huge fangs. Dametrix screamed as he jumped around, trying to brush it off.

As its hairy legs crawled around his left arm it raised its big long fangs like it was about to bite the higher part of his left arm. The bug-like creature pressed down and sank its fangs in his arm. A red light traveled down his arms. Then the creature disappeared.

A voice echoed in his head different from the one he previously heard.

"Hmmm . . . not bad. So you are a human."

There was a rumble and a roar. "Give that back!! It does not belong to you!"

The oak tree grew to more than a hundred feet tall, its roots ripping from the ground. Dametrix and the man looked up as it grew in height. The hole turned into a big mouth with barks sticking out like teeth. "What's going on?" the man yelled. "Give me it now before it grabs you with its branches and twists you over and its mouth drinks your splattered blood."

Getting closer to Dametrix the tree swung its branches around. Sending a cold breeze onto Dametrix's face it swiped the figured man with its branches, sending him flying, screaming, "Damn you, you piece of shhh …" Branches broke, and he heard noises.

Now it seemed to have its big glowing red eyes set on Dametrix. The voice in his head echoed, "Don't worry, you feeble human, I might just enjoy you for a little bit longer. I got this let me at them."

Numerous red lights traveled down Dametrix's left arm like snakes and grew brighter. He raised his left arm higher towards the tree and a huge gun shaped like a bazooka appeared. It fell on his left shoulder. A huge fire blast shot out of the gun and pushed Dametrix backwards.

As the bright light from the gun disappeared, it disintegrated the tree. Dametrix fell to his knees, out of breath, and squeezed his chest near his heart. Sweat dripped from his face to his eyes. He only saw a smoking pathway made by the shot.

Dametrix stumbled to his feet and then saw what looked like a group of men − creatures similar to the one he had encountered before he came out of the darkness. The voice in his head again said, "Don't worry – ha ha ha. I got this. Let me at them." Dametrix looked around and saw more glowing eyes coming towards him.

He ran to where the compass was pointing, and more creatures jumped out of the trees toward him − twenty altogether. Six kept saying, "Let me get them."

Dametrix replied, "No. Last time I used you I ended up almost passing out."

"You humans are such weaklings."

One grabbed him, scratched his leg and tripped him. After rolling on the ground he got up and tried to run faster. A swarm of the man-like creatures landed all around him and circled him. He stood, barely able to see details from a far distance. All he could see were faint movements of heads and arms and glowing eyes. He was surrounded.

Nervous, he yelled, "Look, if I could give you the damn gun I would. I don't even know where it is. Maybe I dropped it. Because I don't have it on me so leave me the hell alone." He looked at them, their mouths open, dripping saliva. The voice in his head screamed, "Let me at them, you foolish impudent sack of meat."

Dametrix yelled, "Fine, just shut up." With a smile on his face he lifted his left arm and pointed it toward them. The closer they were to him the better he could see their teeth and drool. He screamed, "Who's hungry? OK eat this." They showed him their long, sharp nails.

He put his hand down and remembered the pain of being out of breath. "I'm tired of running from cowards like you, picking on a kid. Come on, y'all want a piece of me? Come and get it." They ran toward him.

He jumped and kicked one in the chest with both feet and sent that one creature crashing into the others.

Another jumped on him and he quickly threw him off. It was holding on to him so tightly it left a long scratch mark. He punched and kicked every creature coming towards him, so that his skin was covered in scratches and his clothes were torn and ripped. He pushed them back and   they fell like Dominoes and he stood, covered with scratches, with blood dripping down his eyes and body.

"Ha ha ha ha, what's wrong you cowards? Had enough? I'm more bite than you can chew?"

One of the creatures replied, "Weren't you the one running away like a human? You are only alive because of luck, meat. We are savoring our meal. You're very weak, you can barely stand now. How will you fight? We know you can't use the gun now."

"You roaches dare call me weak, you're the ones who have to sneak around in the shadows. Fighting me in numbers. Afraid to fight me one on one. I would rather die as a human than be a coward like you. I'm not afraid of you stupid things anymore. You should be afraid of me. Who says I can't use the gun? Maybe I'm just saving it for when I get you all in a group like how you are now."

He pointed with his left arm and a light shone off his hand. The creatures backed up.

"By the way you were wrong, you stupid things."

The voice in his head said, "Have respect human. My name is Six."

"OK fine, just get them Six." He had blood in his eyes and he was barely able to see and shot with his left, right, up and down, which stopped the creatures, which were trying to flee.

DMT JOURNEYS

He heard a loud laugh. "You should be ashamed for a human."

As quickly as he heard that was as fast as something hit Dametrix and sent him flying. He found himself floating off the ground. Gasping for air could he barely see from all the blood and sweat dripping in his eyes. An arm reached and grabbed his throat and it choked him. Red eyes glowed. The man choking him said with a high-pitched laugh, "I'll call your bluff, filth. Seeing you like this makes you look like a familiar human." The smile grew wider showing sharp yellow teeth.

"Ah, I remember. You're that kid I was hired to kill. Ha ha ha, guess I'll get to finish you after all."

Holding Dametrix by the throat he looked around at the other dark figures. "Is this what you were all hesitating for? It's just another weak human, a freaking kid."

Dametrix saw a bright light on his right side. He reached out to it. The demon screamed. "Look at me when I'm talking to you. I want you to look into my eyes and see who took your life, remember this name. Devon. For your soul can remember my look and name as I devour it, making you mine. Have it burn in your existence and knowing your soul is mine. What are you staring at? Oh, that damn rusty sword."

Dametrix was a little surprised because he didn't think Devon could see the light coming from it.

"Oh no, nothing will save you this time. I will give you this kid even on your deathbed you are still trying. Since you brought me the gun and my escape out of here I'll grant you a dying request. I'll bring you closer to it."

He slowly lowered Dametrix closer to the sword. As he was about to touch it he quickly brought him back up. "You see that it's the sword of mysteries. Nothing in here can even touch it. It's been said it's a sword of a dead light filth. That's why it rejects us demons and whoever touches it gets burned − or incinerated. Those who are strong enough to even touch it wouldn't even dare try to hold on to it for a long time. Then they would die later. I would say it's the evilest thing here besides that precious gun you're going to give me. Enough already just give me the gun. Or do I have to rip off your arm?"

"OK, pig, fine, touch it. Any choice you make you die at the end, kid."

Dametrix tried to reach out to it but fainted. When he came to, seconds later, he heard laughter but could not see anything. *What's that feeling? It's so warm. It's like I can hear a voice. Is that you Six, or God? Please help me. I promise myself I'll never be a weakling or be in this position again.*

Devon laughed. Others joined in. "Guess we have to do this the hard way. Now let's rip him open and get that gun."

DMT JOURNEYS

Dametrix's eyes glowed white. As Devon tried to use his hand to choke Dametrix his right arm began to glow. The sword flew to Dametrix's right hand and he swung, slicing Devon's left hand. Devon fell to his knees. Blood shot out. Dametrix looked down at Devon with a scolding, angry look.

In a deep voice Dametrix said, "What's wrong?" Devon rose to his feet and tried to back away from him. "Don't back up where not finish here."

He disappeared and reappeared, kicking Devon to the floor. Devon was shocked. "This makes no sense. How are you able to hold the sword?"

"Shut up and tell me what would make a roach like you try to kill a helpless fifteen-year-old boy sleeping on his bed."

"Ha ha ha. I see now why they want you dead. Don't think just because you're not dying in my arms like the weak human you will always be that you won. I see from the steam coming out your hand the sword rejects you. It's just a matter of time before it kills you."

"You said 'they.' That means there's more than one. Now tell me their names."

"I'm not telling you a damn thing. You're nothing but food to me. Doesn't look that way up here where I'm standing. Why don't you look into my eyes now?"

Dametrix gripped the sword with both hands and swung hard over Devon. A huge hole opened up.

Demons watched him on his left. They came after him and he quickly turned around and fell in the black hole. He bounced and then hit the ground. As he tried to get up, he reached and felt something soft.

It was a bed. Next to a clock.

"What are you doing down there, boy, making all that noise?"

He smiled. "Nothing Grandma. Ummm, just finished painting my room."

He fell on his bed and passed out.

He heard a knock, got up and ran outside, thinking it was like the last time when he met David. The bright sun nearly blinded him. A girl wearing a black shirt and black pants stared at him. It was Derica. With a confusing, yet satisfying, look on her face she said, "Cool tattoos. You
must have some really cool parents."

Dametrix said, "What are you talking about?"

"Your shoulders are real, right? Or did you do it to yourself? Looks like you have been bleeding. Are you OK? I see marks on you, is it paint? What's going on with your clothes? Your boxers are showing, by the way."

Dametrix, embarrassed, tried to cover up with his hand. "No, no, no, I'm, um fine. Aren't you Derica, the one dating Sam?"

"Is that what he's telling everyone? No we are not."

"Oh yeah, you turned him down?"

"Aren't you one of his friends he hangs around with or used to? I thought I recognized you. You look different." They stared at each other for a moment. "Well I just wanted to let you know that your dog is barking a lot. Is he OK?"

Dametrix replied, "What dog?"

"Don't you hear it? Come here Mr. Rip pants, I'll show you. He's in your parking lot."

"Thank you Miss, um... I appreciate it so, so much."

"Can you call me Derica? Not miss and I'm not dating Sam. You can tell him to stop spreading rumors."

"I'm Dametrix. I didn't mean that because he didn't even say that. I know you're the quiet girl that sits in the front. What are you doing here? I'm not saying you can't be here, I'm just wondering."

"Ha, ha. You're funny I live right over there. I always see you running to the bus stop like you're always late. I already told you I came here for the dog to stop barking. Must belong to the other neighbors. What happened to you? You look like you fell into a shredding machine or got beat up."

He stuttered a bit. "What? No. I know how to fight. I can beat up a hundred people. Everyone respects me. Everyone fears me. I'm...not afraid of anything. I was just painting my room. I fell and landed on my feet 'cause, you know, I'm strong with cat-like reflexes. The bucket of paint fell but I karate-kicked it and some splashed on me."

"Right. But that doesn't explain how your clothes got ripped."

He heard his grandmother call his name, which made him jump.

"Um...I have to go. My grandma is calling me. Not that she controls me, she just needs my help lifting some heavy boxes."

Derica blushed. "If you say so." She reached in her pocket and pulled out a little pink pen with a scratch image of a unicorn on it. With a white-faded recipe paper she wrote down her number.

"Before you leave here's my number, you know, just to tell me about what actually happened. Or how you got your clothes ripped, tough guy. I'd love to hear the end of this story. By the way nice tattoos."

"What tattoos?" He looked at his arm and then noticed a mark on both his shoulders. Responding   to her confused reaction, he said, "Thanks, I'm thinking about getting more is what I meant.

His heart rushing, he took the number and walked away. They both turned and waved good-bye.

He reached his house and thought about his grandma and what she would say if she saw the tattoos. Visions of her chasing him with a belt came to his mind. He took a gulp and walked inside with his hands across his shoulder, trying to cover up.

"Stop right there, boy," his grandma shouted. He almost made it to his room.

"What is it Grandma?" He turned slowly to make sure she could not see the front of his body.

"What you got there?"

He turned a little bit more. "Nothing. Just a piece of paper. I just got the phone number of that girl …"

"And what happened to your clothes?"

"I was painting in the room and the bucket kinda fell."

"Is that why you made that noise last night?"

And it all came rushing back to him. *It can't be real, can it?* "Um...yeah, Grandma. I was going to take a shower and get all this paint off me."

"Did you make a mess in that room boy?"

"No, Grandma, I know better. You would beat my butt."

"You got that right, now hurry and clean up. Look up when you are talking to people."

He had been staring at the floor and when he looked up he realized she was wearing her favorite shirt, with the words Number One Grandma, the one he bought for her birthday. She hadn't worn that in a while. She looked younger, but still old with all her white hair.

DMT JOURNEYS

She smiled. "I made your favorite breakfast. Go ahead and get cleaned up."

He walked into the bathroom and could not believe what he was seeing in the mirror. A big number six, with red outlines around it on his left shoulder and the number seven on his right shoulder with yellow outlines around it. *I can't believe she didn't see it.*

In the shower the water turned dark blood red just for a minute.

He thought about the night before, the fight, and how he finally met the one haunting his dreams, Devon. And how he got his revenge and ended up back in his room. *Maybe this won't be so bad. I'll be the coolest kid in school with not one, but two tattoos. And apparently I have powers. What kid can say that? Oh man, I can't wait for school to start. I'll pick out the best outfit for school.*

He wiped the condensation from the mirror – there were no scratches on him, just white streaks from the front of his hair to the middle of his head. *I can't believe this is real. All the cuts are gone. I don't even feel the pain anymore. Maybe I can heal fast.*

Back in his bedroom he retrieved a pair of scissors from his dresser.

If I cut myself maybe I can heal fast. Does that mean Bruce is real too? Then that means I can't show my power like he said.

The number six on his shoulder started to glow bright red. A voice echoed in his head, "Is whining all you ever do?"

"Who said that?" *Oh man, I'm losing my mind.*

I forgot about that great food Grandma made. Today is going to be a good day. I'm not going to let nothing mess it up. Gram Gram is here. Finally, she made her awesome food. I'm sure she wants to watch a movie like we used to before she started working so much.

He started out the door but went back to his room, grabbed a long-sleeve shirt and put on short jeans. While looking at himself getting dressed in the mirror the number six on his shoulder started to glow again. He decided to put on a jacket.

Let's see you glow now.

He stepped outside his room and entered the kitchen. His grandma wanted him to eat and watch a movie. "You want to watch the one about the guy with powers?" "Yes." He quickly ran to the table.

"It's been awhile since we had movie time together," she said while he stuffed his face. With a sad, yet proud look on her face, almost as if she wants to cry, she says, "I know that I haven't been here like I used to. You know I'm working double for us, right? It's not that I don't love you."

"I know, Grandma. You do it so we can have all these things and I love you too.

She smiled and added, "I'm sure your body is going through some changes."

"Oh my gosh, no Grandma, can we not do that?"

She laughs hysterically. "You don't even know what I'm about to say. It's not what you think. I was going to talk about your p—"

Suddenly there was a knock on the door. "I got it!" Dametrix opened the door to see Stanly and Martino, both with goofy smiles.

Stanly laughed. "What's the matter stupid? You couldn't decide if you were cold or hot?"

He slammed the door. "Oh, come on," he heard them yelling. "It was a joke."

"Hey you want to come outside and play or are you going to blow us off like you always do?" He opened the door slightly and they forced themselves inside, calling for "Grandma Sunday," which they nicknamed her because every Sunday she made a big dinner to celebrate after church. Because Sunday is the beginning of the week and the day to rest.

She looked at Dametrix. "You've been avoiding your friends boy?"

"No ma'am I just been busy but I'm about to go out and play if it's OK with you."

"Sure. What about the movie? And you didn't finish eating your food."

"We can watch the movie when I come back. I wouldn't miss it for anything." He ran outside and hit Stanly on the back of his head.

"Ow, what the hell is that for?"

"Don't say hell and that's for trying to be a smart ass and snitching on me to my grandma."

"So, I can't say hell, but you can say ass? What are you some backwards saint now?"

"No, I just don't like the word anymore."

"Why the hell not?"

"It's a dope word."

"I like it, so get the hell out of here with that pastor stuff Dametrix. If I wanted to feel bad about what I'm doing, I would be in church."

Seeing the look on Dametrix's face, Stanly ran and Dametrix ran after him, reaching him in seconds. He slapped Stanly in the back of the head again. "Ha, I got you, slow poke."

"What? How did you do that? I must have been at least a block away from you."

Martino was panting hard. "Wow, dude. That was really cool. How did you run so fast? It looks like there was dust behind you, almost like you disappeared on the sidewalk."

"It's probably from chasing the bus all those damn times," Stanly said. "Are you hiding something from me again? Come to think of it, you do look different. You look bigger, and what's with the damn jacket? Take it off."

"I don't want to. I'm cold."

"It's freaking October, the cold hasn't started yet. If you're cold, why do you have shorts on? I think you're lying. Ow, what was that?"

They both looked around.

"Did you guys see that? It felt like something was trying to trip me," Martino said while looking around.

"We've taken this short cut in the alley for as long as I can remember – you never tripped here before," Dametrix said. "Come on let's go."

Martino couldn't move. "It feels like something is grabbing me," Martino said.

Dametrix moved towards him to find what was holding him. "What's wrong, buddy? What's got you? I don't see anything."

"Please Dutch help me," Martino said with a petrified look on his face. "I'm scared now."

Dametrix, panicked and angry, couldn't find what was holding him.

Then Martino started to levitate. He looked down at Dametrix as Dametrix tried to pull him down, feeling powerless at not being able to help. He was the youngest, like their kid brother and he had always promised to protect him, no matter what. He started to run and Stanly followed after him.

DMT JOURNEYS

Martino screamed, "No guys, please don't leave me here by myself."

"We're going to find someone to help you," Dametrix yelled and grabbed Stanly. There was so much fear in his eyes – he had never seen Stanly this way, all the times they had gotten into trouble including the times with Martino.

Sitting in the principal's office, the police station, always trying to look like the cool, mellow guy.

"Go back, keep an eye on him," Dametrix said to Stanly.

"I can't do anything by myself," Stanly said. Dametrix shook him and screamed, "What would Sam do if he was here? He would be ashamed to see you."

Stanly said, "OK, I should go get Sam. He would know what to do."

"I've wasted enough time." Dametrix ran and Stanly chased him, with every second getting farther and farther away. He got closer to his home and thought that Stanly might be right, Sam wouldn't want him to run. He would try to figure something out. He heard a maniacal laugh that got louder. "What was that?"

"You're running away when your friends ask for help."

"Who said that? Show yourself!"

"It's so pitiful how you humans are in such denial when you know the truth inside of you. That's right, the gun and the glasses, they're all inside of me.

So this whole time the gun has been talking. No guns don't talk. Maybe it's an evil spirit.

Running as fast as he could back to Martino, Dametrix hoped it wasn't too late and that he would know how to use that gun. He headed back to shortcut ally. Gone were Stanly and Martino. It was just an empty ally. He ran past the ally. Nothing. He leaned against the wall. Oh man, what do I do now? What about their moms? I have to tell them.

Maybe they went back to their house and they're waiting for me.

Yeah, I wish I was that lucky.

The whole way Dametrix tried to figure out a way to tell Martino's mom that her only son was taken by a demon monster.

"This is going to be so hard," he said to himself. He reached the door and imagined all her reactions: "I hate you. A demon? Are you serious? This is your fault, how could you? You were supposed to be his friend and look out for him, you coward."

He knocked twice. The sound was like someone hammering a nail in his coffin. His heart raced.

"Who is it?" she yelled out.

Dametrix opened his mouth. It felt so dry. "It's me, Dametrix."

She opened the door, a confused look on her face. "Oh hey, Dametrix, what are you doing here? Is everything OK? I thought you went home."

"No, I have to tell you something, it's not easy for me to say it but … something happened to Martino. I think he was taken."

"Stop playing around. Martino's here."

Martino walked towards the door.

"Oh man, you're OK," Dametrix said. "Come here, buddy. Give me a hug."

Martino stayed where he was, looking stiff as a board.

"Are you mad at me? I didn't run to leave you alone. You should know I would never do that to you."

Martino stood with a blank stare.

"I had to go get something so I could help you out, then I remembered I didn't need it," Dametrix said.

"What was so important you left me and when did you realize you didn't need it?" Martino said.

"Well it's a little complicated. I can't say really. Well. I'm not supposed to."

"Yeah. Whatever. You and your secrets and lies."

The number six on his left shoulder glowed and flashed. He heard a voice: "Tell him the truth. Tell him, human." He recalled Bruce's words: *Don't ever reveal your abilities. Don't reveal yourself to anyone for any reason.*

"Well, I'm waiting. Hello? Why are you just covering your ears and looking down? I'm talking to you Dutch."

 Dametrix said, "I'll see you at school."

Out on the sidewalk he bumped into Stanly.

"Whoa, where are you going?" Stanly said. "And where did you run off to?"

Dametrix gave him an angry look. "Me? What about you? Where did you go?" He balled his fingers into a fist and then looked back and saw Martino, saying, "Leave him alone you ran, too."

"Why are you in such a rush? Did you find Martino?"

"Isn't he behind me?"

"No. No one's there."

"Then he's in his house."

"That's good. You found him. You don't seem so happy. Where did you go? I couldn't find you. Did you find what you ran off to go look at? Come on let's go see if Martino is OK."

Stanly ran towards Martino's house. Dametrix watched them hug, happy to see each other.

How happy Martino is to see Stanly. He doesn't even like being with him that much. He probably doesn't see him as a coward like he sees me, I bet he's probably mad at me. Maybe that's why he gave me that blank look. I'm losing all my friends because of these secrets. Maybe I should let them know. I mean, they're my friends. It's not like I'm telling strangers. I'm sure that's what Bruce was trying to say. We don't hold secrets from each other. We told each other we wouldn't.

"Yeah human, go ahead. See how much better you will feel."

"Hey guys. I have something to tell you. OK, I ran off to go get these glasses to be able to see what was holding you. I think It was a demon. I don't know but then I realized that I have a gun and I can shoot it."

"Whoa, wait. You have a gun?"

"Forget that," Martino said. "He said he has glasses that see demons."

"You're just making up lies and stories," Martino said. "A little bit too much running got you light-headed. Do you need to go take a nap, princess? You know you do need sixteen hours of beauty sleep."

"Ha ha ha ha," Stanley said. "Yeah, go get your magical glasses and go back in time with Santa Claus and save Christmas."

Dametrix raised his left hand towards Stanly.

"Oh, is that your gun? Let me guess. It's invisible and powered by your imagination. Well I have a gun too. It's powered by your mom. Want to give it a try?" He let out a laugh.

A red beam shot out from Dametrix's arm. Out came Six with a burst of light.

Smoke came from the barrel of the gun. Stanly froze, shock on his face. Martino had a surprised, yet satisfied look on his face.

"OK, we believe you," Stanly said. "Just put it down."

"Hey, what are you guys doing?" It was Martino's mom yelling from the house. Dametrix quickly hid his hand.

Stanly put his hands down, watching a little light coming off of Dametrix's left shoulder. It was visible through the shirt and the jacket.

"Nothing Mom, go back inside," Martino said.

"Don't tell me it's nothing. Let me see your hands." She walked closer. "Show me your hands now. Show me."

She grabbed Dametrix's hands. Nothing was there. "Where is it? You had a gun pointed at his face. Where are you hiding it?"

"It wasn't a gun. It was my finger. We were playing cops and robbers."

"Yeah, we were   playing freeze tag," Martino said.

"Well, which one was it that you guys were playing?
Don't lie to me."

Dametrix replied, "Well it was cops and robbers. If you get caught or tagged you have to freeze." He smiled nervously while looking at Martino's mom, scared of the angry look she was giving him.

She turned to go back into the house. "Finish up. You guys have ten minutes left."

Martino followed his mom and said to Stanly, "See you later.'

When she was gone, Stanly said, "What was that? Did you see that menacing look he gave me saying bye? And why did he say he'd see me later, but not you?"

"I think he was just saying bye. You're putting too much into this."

"How did you get that gun? It's so cool. Is that how you were able to kick that bully's butt? When he was bullying that kid is that what you were doing? You just tell us you just been sleeping?" Then he thought about it a bit more. "Wait. Is that what happened when you had that nightmare? Did you and the demon become one? Now you have powers like in the movies? Oh my gosh, that's so cool. Can I have powers too?"

"Whoa, whoa, whoa," Dametrix said. "Relax. It's a long story. I'll tell you later. I'll be waiting for you at school."

That night Dametrix had a horrible nightmare about Martino attacking Derica and ripping out her heart. While Stanly stood there, smiling.

Dametrix tried to run to save her but it seemed the closer he got the farther they were. He woke in a sweat, holding a glowing sword in his hand that disappeared in the blink of an eye. The alarm rang.

"Oh no. I'm late. That's the final alarm." He quickly got dressed. "How stupid. How could I miss the first alarm?" He looked outside and saw the bus driving away.

"I hate this damn alarm clock. The damn bus couldn't wait longer. All the days in the week you pick today to come early. If my grandma was here to wake me up like everyone else's parents . . . nah, I love my grandma, I take it back. Damn universe hates me. I bet God is just laughing in his chair at my life."

Outside he ran toward the bus and it seemed all the noise of the cars went quiet. *Bam!* The bus stopped suddenly, and he ran smack into it, face first. He fell backward and looked up to see a girl looking at him. Was it an angel?

"You're pretty," he said.

The others on the bus laughed.

"You OK Dutch?" the bus driver said. "Please be OK."

"Yeah I'm good," he said and got up. "Why wouldn't I be good?" He brushed himself off and noticed Derica looking at him. "Where am I?" The bus had parked in front of the school. "How did I get to school already?"

"That's what I would like to know," the bus driver said. "Your house is about five miles from the school. Three if you take the shortcut which I didn't, 'cause all the lights were green so I kept going straight all the way until I got to the school. I was doing about thirty-five miles an hour because I was about to be late waiting for you. Cause you're always late to get on the bus. I even saved you for last."

"That's why you're the best," Dametrix said. Everyone laughed.

"OK, get to your class kids."

Dametrix began walking toward the school and noticed Stanly and Martino watching him.

"Hey dude are you OK?" Sam said.

The class bell rang. Dametrix started running and everyone yelled at him, saying they were going to be late because of him.

The bus driver said, "Don't blame him. What did I tell you guys to do? Bunch of hard-headed kids."

In class, Dametrix was trying to figure out how to make the guys stop being angry at him.

I'll just tell them I made it up or that it's a secret. That I'm taking karate and the teacher told me to keep it a secret. Yeah that's easy enough and it's not lying, technically. Ha ha they will think it's so cool I know how to fight and it will explain how I beat up the bully.

He laughed to himself. The teacher told him to quiet down. "Why don't you tell me the square root of pie?" the teacher said.

The school bell rang.

DMT JOURNEYS

"Um, it's whatever flavor the pie is. I would love to answer but that's the bell for lunch time."

"All right everyone, don't forget to do your homework. That includes you to Mr. Dametrix. Be safe over the weekend. I won't be here for a couple of days."

He ran to the cafeteria and grabbed a cheeseburger for lunch. *Yeah, it's going to be an awesome weekend. School is about to close soon. Man, time is flying by fast.*

He got his food and walked to where his friends and Sam were sitting.

"Whoa, what are you doing here?" he said to Sam. "I thought you were supposed to be at boot camp."

"They changed it again since I did that program. My parents said they wanted me to finish school here after I got into a fight with them. Now I get to spend time with my best friends." Sam sarcastically added, "Yay, boot camp over the summer. "Then football or basketball tryouts, depending on which scholarship my parents think is better.

He whispered to Dametrix, "Hey before I forget. Are we still going to check out the haunted house? Can you do it today? Awe, don't tell me you forgot. I heard you can do some cool stuff. It will help us out on our hunt."

Damn, I did forget. What's with this guy and where does he get all that energy? Who wants to go investigate a scary haunted house that's some white people TV stuff? Where we always die first.

DMT JOURNEYS

"Yeah, buddy, of course I didn't forget. What cool stuff are you talking about and who told you about it? Never mind, I'm sure I can guess."

Stanly stared at Dametrix. "Well, show us this cool trick." Everyone joined in. Dametrix cried out, "Really, you told all these people?"

"Oh my gosh, you're just trying to get out of it again." Stanly replied. "I knew you were lying probably. You ran home to your grandma crying leaving poor little Martino by himself."

"That's not what happened," Dametrix said. "Shut up. I already told you the truth."

"If it's true, prove it," Martino said.

"Yeah, Dutch, prove you're not a liar," Stanly said.

"OK guys leave him alone," Sam said in a deep, fatherly voice. "If he says it's true, as his friends we should believe him."

"Show them, human, show them. Stop being weak."

Dametrix rose to leave and balled his hand into a fist while looking at everyone around him chanting, "Show us!" while banging on the table. His left hand was glowing, and he raised it to Stanly in a huge, white flash. Everyone stood with their mouths open. Stanly fell backwards from his seat.

The other students enjoying their lunch left their tables and ran towards Dametrix and his friends.

DMT JOURNEYS

Dametrix's eyes changed from black and red then back to normal and the red faded. "I'm sorry," he said. "I didn't really mean it."

"Ha ha, it's fine, man," Stanly said. Dametrix helped him to his feet.

"You really do have a magic gun. Wow. Bring it back out again."

Everyone wanted to see the gun.

"It's too late now, human, they already know and seen me. You have no other choice but to do it."

Dametrix opened his left palm, where a light beamed. The veins in his arms glowed red and a light showed all the veins in his arm glowing red. The gun flashed with number six imprinted on it with.

Little Six connected, creating a larger number six on the grip of the gun. Everyone was shocked and amazed and crowded around him.

Six echoed in his head, "Go on take your shirt off. You're one of the cool kids."

Dametrix took his shirt off. Sounds of shock reverberated across the room. His body ripped, his tattoos glowing. Girls rushed to him, saying, "Oh my gosh that's so hot," followed by jealous boyfriends giving him the stink eye as they walked away, bumping into him.

Everyone wanted to be like him and Dametrix smiled as he thought to himself, *This must be how Sam feels every day. Is this what it's like to be the cool guy? I feel like a star. All the girls reaching out to you. People want to be your friend.*

Stanly and Martino were pushed out of the crowd. "What a jerk," Stanly said.

"First he ignores us now this. He is some friend," Martino said.

"Oh, come on guys, leave him alone. Let him enjoy his moment," Sam said. "Since I've known him, he was always the quiet kid that always tried to help people out. I'm sure if it was you Stanley you would do the same. Or you Martino."

"You're only saying that because this is what it's like for you every day, Sam. Since we've known you, you've always been the popular kid since middle school, now high school. I bet you were popular in elementary school too, probably even in your mom's stomach. All the nurses gathered around. From the looks of it he might become more popular than you or stronger than you."

"OK, half of that is true; the rest you stole from that song, 'I'm Not That Bad to the Bone.' And he's not that much bigger; it's 'cause he's shorter. That's why it looks that way."

"Come on guys, be happy for him. Who helped you out when your mom died, Stanly, or when your dad died, Martino? It was always him and I'm not going to lie. He helped me out a lot, too."

DMT JOURNEYS

"Yeah, every time a girl is looking for you to beat you up he always lied for you. Ha ha it happened one time. No, remember the Hispanic girl with the knife? Yeah and the Asian one who brings the nunchucks to school? We told you to stay away from a girl who's in karate. What about the white girl who became friends with the black girl just to beat you up?"

Sam said, "Fine. I get the point."

After lunch Dametrix was sitting in class, enjoying his new-found fame, when the intercom came on.

"Will Dutch Dametrix please come to my office now."

"You know it's serious," someone whispered to the class. "He didn't even call the teacher on her phone."

Dametrix left in a panic. *Oh my gosh I'm in trouble now. Having a gun in school. I could go to jail for years.* His hands were shaking.

He opened the door to the principal's office, hearing every creak of the door, smelling a mingling of office supplies and air freshener.

"Come right in, Mr. Dametrix, have a seat. I've been hearing rumors about you. I'm sure you have an idea why you're here."

Dametrix sat and played with his fingers.

"You look different since I've last seen you. How's your nice grandma doing?"

"Um… she's OK. Been working."

"Was she the one who let you get those tattoos? She knows you have them?"

"No sir."

"Is it true you brought a gun to school? Listen here, Dametrix, is there something you want to talk about? The two years you've been at this school I've never really had big problems with you. You get to school late and you're a class clown sometimes, which I'm sure has to do with being around that interesting friend of yours, Mr. Sterly, or Stanly, whichever one he's calling himself. Almost makes me feel bad for Martino Demanche. Despite all of that I figured you guys always look out for each other and keep each other out of trouble. Especially Mr. Sam. Last I heard you guys aren't getting along that well or aren't even hanging out anymore.

"Don't leave your friends for the wrong crowd, there's a lot of kids in gangs throwing their future away. I look at it as you did that for your friends, and they did the same for you. I'm sorry we had to search your locker. They found nothing, which I am glad to hear. Your book bag is being searched. This is a serious matter. I have to follow rules. Now I'm asking you because there's other things I will have to do. I rather just ask you to be honest with me. I'm sure you have never lied to me, right?"

DMT JOURNEYS

"Yes sir, I do appreciate you always helping me. You don't have to worry. I don't have a gun."

"OK, just know I do have my eye on you next time you come in here or if we found out you lied. I will have to expel you from this school – or worse – which I don't want to do."

He looked Dametrix squarely in the eyes. "I want to tell you a story. There was a little bird in a tree on a cold night. The bird couldn't fly yet and its parents disappeared. The bird moved and moved until it fell down the tree onto the cold ground. It started yelling peep peep peep! A cow passing by heard the bird. And felt sorry for it, so the cow lifted its tail and dropped a hot cow pie splat on the bird. Now the little bird was all warm and snuggled in the poo. He looked around and started yelling *peep peep peep.* Then a wolf comes by and lifts the bird up high, dusts him off nice and clean, puts him in his mouth and swallows the bird whole.

"If you can figure out what that story means you will learn a great lesson in life."

"Thank you, Principal. That's why you're my favorite principal of them all."

Looking up, he said "thank you" to God and walked back to class. One the way he bumped into Derica as he turned a corner in the hall. "Oh my gosh, I'm so sorry, I didn't see you. Please don't be mad."

"It's OK. I wanted to ask you something but you had your group of followers and I didn't get a chance to," she said. "Me and a couple of my friends are getting something to eat at the mall. Want to come?"

"YES. I mean yeah, yeah, sure, that's cool, whatever."

"Ha ha, yeah, way to keep it smooth. Just text me."

"Yeah, I forgot to text you. I'm sorry."

"It's fine. I thought I gave you the wrong one. That's why you never texted me. But it's OK, I lost my phone." She gave him her new number.

"You are not going to blow me off again, right?" she said. "I didn't think so. See you after school."

Back at class it was evident he was missed. He looked at his classmates with an arrogant smirk.

"Dutch, you're back," one of them said.

"Of course, did ya miss me?"

After school he was so excited about meeting Derica that he ran to the mall. He gave himself a running start and focused on what he had been learning, and then he sprinted. His heart was so filled with excitement that he yelled out and an aura surrounded him. He screamed as everything moved in slow motion. "This is so cool,' he said to himself.

DMT JOURNEYS

174

He reached the mall in an instant, bought a sleeveless V-neck in one of the stores and went to the bathroom and changed his shirt. He washed his face and looked in the mirror, for once not caring that his hair was looking whiter.

He texted Derica.

Hey I'm at the mall where are you?

Derica:

I'm at the food court next to the Sub Hut by the pizza kiosk. How did you get here so fast ? Didn't school just end? Do you not have a final period like me?

He ran and when he got close he slowed down and began walking nonchalantly. His face changed when he saw her.

"Oh hey, Dutch, you made it. Want anything to eat? These are my brothers and sister. That pretty girl over there is Wei Xian. Call her Wei Ji and that guy with the mustache is Elrico Pablo Loco. And that pretty boy over there is our older brother, Alexander, or Nopa, short for Napoleon. Everyone, this is Dutch, the guy I was telling you about."

Dutch waved nervously and wanted to look tough beside the college-looking kids with grown facial hair. He sat down next to Derica and before too long the rest got up and left.

"Where are they going? I was enjoying their company."

She laughed. "No, you weren't. I saw that nervous look in your face. They have stuff to do. Besides, I wanted it to be just me and you.."

"OK. I like your idea."

She said, "I bet you get all the girls seeing how you're so popular in school."

"No, I'm just a normal guy. I have no girl."

"I find that hard to believe. You have muscles. You hang out with Sam and you have tattoos. You have a cool trick you do with a gun, too."

"Oh, you heard about that? No, it's just a silly thing. I only like one girl who I was thinking about. Not that I'm a weirdo who thinks about her a lot. I think about other things like football and wrestling. I think about girl sports too. I'm not sexist or gay. Not that there's anything wrong with it. I believe everyone should have their own choices."

She put a finger to his lips. "You're really funny. So what girl did you have in mind? Was it my sister? Everyone thinks she's pretty. Gorgeous. Hot."

"Not as pretty as you." They leaned in closer.

"You're cute too," she said.

DMT JOURNEYS

His phone rang. It was Sam. "Hey, buddy, what's up man? Where are you?"

"I wanted to figure out how we're doing this since we didn't get to talk much about it. I'm heading to the house now. You can meet me there."

Oh no, damn, I should have never picked up. "Hey Sam, I'm here at the mall with Derica."

"OK, it's cool, I understand. Go ahead, you lucky dog you. Good luck. Not that you need it since you have your new popularity."

Feeling badly, Dametrix said, "Wait. I'll meet you there in a little bit."

"You sure? You don't have to meet me at the spooky scary house where me, your best friend is going to be all by himself alone."

"I just said I'd meet you there. I made a promise and I'll stick to it. Besides you're always there for me, man. I'll be there in a few."

"The most I'll wait is twenty minutes."

"I'll be at the house in an hour."

Sam made a smooching noise to mock Dametrix. "Don't forget. Give her a kiss for me and let me know how it was, ha ha ha."

"Everything OK Dametrix?" Derica said as he ended the call. "You look a little worried."

"No, it's fine. So back to what we were doing. I think our faces were about to do something together."

DMT JOURNEYS

She smiled. "I like talking to you. I feel like we connect, like I can just trust you."

He leaned in for a kiss and she backed away and changed the subject. "How did you learn that trick, really?" "I just did some research on the internet to learn it that way."

"Can you do any other things? Can you show me how?"

"Hey, did you just invite me here to ask about my tricks?"

"No, not really I just think it's cool how you can do that." She tried to kiss him while he tried to get up. Then she pulled him closer and kissed him.

"I've been saying I have to go for the past couple of minutes and now I really have to go."

"Why? Can't you stay so we can talk more? Maybe you can show me." She rubbed his left arm.

He took her hand away from his shirt. "No, I'm going to go. You seem like everyone else. You just care about my arm."

"No, it's not true. I meant those things I said to you Dametrix. Just sit down and we'll talk."

"I'm leaving, bye. I've stayed longer than I should."

He raced to the haunted house. He reached the back of the mall and ran as fast as he could. I *hope Sam isn't mad.* He reached the house and saw no one. He passed through the broken rusted fence and walked to the front door, through the tall grass. The house appeared to be at least a hundred years old. *I see why they call this the house of death. Looks like it died. How come they haven't destroyed this thing?*

He stared at the house, getting the sense that someone stared back at him. Oh man, I hope this isn't the Amityville house. It looks just like it.

He opened the front door and heard creaking from what sounded like other doors. The room was taken up with a few chairs. There was dust everywhere and spider webs in every corner. The floor creaked with each step.

Dametrix whispered, "Sam, where are you? This place is creepy." He headed toward the kitchen and saw a clear streak from the dusty, dirty floor and followed it to the basement. He opened the door slowly, holding Six in his hand.

In the basement, a bit of light came from one of the windows and he saw what appeared to be red sneakers. "Hey Sam, if you're trying to scare me, stop it, man, it isn't funny." He headed down the creaking steps and at the bottom the image became clearer. There was a leg attached to the sneakers. He moved closer and spotted black basketball shorts with the letters "QH."

He screamed and rushed to the body. "Oh, no, wake up Sam. Wake up."

There was blood on Sam's lifeless body. Dutch screamed even louder. Six on his shoulder started to glow. He looked up to hear a man speaking in the distance.

"This is the NYPD. Anybody still in here? We received a call about a breaking and entering. We heard a scream. Is anyone in here hurt?"

The cop spotted the basement door open from the front door as he approached the basement. He felt a heavy weight pushing on him, which slowed him down. After finally reaching the basement door the cop looked down and saw Dametrix 's back turn as he knelt on the floor, holding the body. He was shaking Sam with his left hand while right hand held Six.

Six said to Dametrix, "Now is the time to run human."

"Freeze," the cop said. "Turn around slowly. Put your hands up and drop the weapon slowly and come towards me."

In a deep voice, Dametrix said, "My friend needs help while getting up."

"Drop the gun. This is the last warning or I will shoot you."

"It's not a gun, it's a toy."

"Run you, stupid human."

The cop was talking into his radio. "I have a ten eightyfive and ten eighty-seven with possible one eighty-seven."

Dametrix raised his aura and the cop fell and fired a shot and then looked up. Dametrix was gone. He ran all the way home, thinking about how he nearly missed the bullet passing by his face. As his best friend remained on the floor. He went to his room and took off his bloody shirt.

"Oh man, if only I would have gotten there sooner. Maybe Bruce can help me reverse time. I'm sure if I explain it he will. I need to sleep."

He looked in his drawers, moved everything around, then threw all the contents on the floor. Then he had an idea. *I could knock myself out. I just need to sleep!* He banged his head against the wall, and it made a huge hole. Because of his training he realized he could take the beating he banged his head multiple times.

A white, empty void appeared. Dametrix yelled, "Bruce you in here?"

"Who is that? Dametrix is that you? Where have you been? You look different, kid."

"I know, everyone has been telling me that. I need you to teach me how to go back in time. You said you can do it, right?"

A troubled look crossed Bruce's face. "What's wrong? What happened and why do you need to go back in time? Usually when someone wants to change time it's because of something they could have done or wanted to do to change it. It's never good. You need to understand that time is a very delicate and complicated thing, kid. Whatever happened is meant to happen and happen for a reason."

Dametrix grabbed Bruce by his collar. "What did you just say? "I don't have time for your fortune cookie crap. Please just teach me how to do it. My friend just died and it's my fault."

"I can't do that kid. Changing the past won't help. It might just create a more dangerous situation."

"Ahhh I'm so tired of your BS. I ask you to do one thing for me."

Bruce appeared worried and grabbed Dametrix's left sleeve while watching him slowly starting to levitate, which created a shadow under him that grew larger by the minute.

Dametrix's voice deepened. "Get your hands off me old man." He tried to pull away from Bruce, who gripped him and ripped his shirt sleeve, revealing the number six on his shoulder.

"How did you get that mark on your shoulder?"

Dametrix yelled, "That's not what i came here for. Are you going to help me or not?"

Bruce screamed, "You don't even know what it is, do you? It's a curse mark kid. We have to remove it from your arm before it's too late."

"I'm tired of your lectures. All you want me to do is hide. Holding me back like the voice said. You never really helped me out. You've only helped yourself."

"How could you say that? I taught you to defend yourself and tried to guide you to have a better future. I taught you to think before you act so you can make better life choices. Every choice has its consequences, kid. I even sent you to get a powerful weapon."

Dametrix replied, "Your stupid gun didn't even work. I got pushed out of the portal by a big blast and found something better."

"That's not possible, it shouldn't be, was that how you got the curse mark? Look at what you're letting happen kid. Control yourself before it's too late."

"Everything you said was wrong, I showed my power and nothing bad happened. All it did was show me the truth, that you're just a lonely old miserable fool and you just wanted me to be like you."

A hand emerged from the huge shadow that was cast from underneath Dametrix. Then a dark figure climbed out of the shadow and stood oozing black slime that fell on the floor like tar. It was a demon creature with green skin and sharp teeth. Bruce kicked it back in the shadow. More came out and the swarm charged at Bruce.

Dametrix lowered himself and a dark figure grabbed his leg and tried to pull him into the dark shadow pool. Dametrix tried to bring out his six gun but he couldn't.

Maybe I can't use it in this dream world or whatever this is. He kicked the black bob and kicked in an attempt to fight off the slime creatures. Bruce grabbed him.

"What are you doing? Let go of me Bruce."

Bruce stared at him. "You have to let me take care of this."

The portal opened and he threw Dametrix towards it. A bright blast came out of Dametrix's right arm.

Then Dametrix opened his eyes and found he was back in his own room. He needed to go to sleep but he knew he would not be able to without help

"I have to get Bruce out of it. He needs my help. I'm not going to lose someone else today because of me." He searched his room and his bathroom for sleeping pills and then ran into his grandma's bedroom where she was sleeping. If he could get sleeping pills from her to let him sleep that would help.

"Grandma, please don't be mad. Can I get some sleeping pills?" He turned on the light.

He rolled her over onto her back and saw red on the bed and sheets on her stomach and face. Tears fell onto his face and he started to shake as Six appeared in his left hand. Her mouth was covered in blood. She was wearing a shirt he got for her – her favorite shirt.

"We were supposed to watch a movie together and I went from being barely able to see you to never again going to see you."

He screamed. The house shook even more.

The police came to the house. *How?* Dametrix thought. A neighbor must have called them because of all the noise. Two of them walked into the home and tried to come up the stairs. Every step seemed to be harder and heavier. Officer Rick, obviously more athletic than the others, was the first up the stairs and said into his radio, "I'm going to need lots of back up from any available units. Bill, I think this is what you were talking about earlier."

When he got to the door it seemed to Dametrix that his breathing was labored.

"Freeze kid. Drop the gun now."

He looked at the cop that's trying to stand and the room shook again.

"I could kill him if I wanted to. He's just a weakling. He can barely stand up in my presence." human let me at them Six continued to talk. "Yes. It's really easy. I'll help you."

"Do it. No one would know."

"Drop the gun and get down on the ground now." The cop stared at Dametrix with an angry expression on his face. Drop the gun now this is your final warning.

Dametrix's eyes glowed and he appeared to have a maniacal look on his face as if he was smiling with an evil smile.

"It's not a gun, it's a toy, you weakling." The cop was barely able to hold up his gun and fired one shot to the right, hitting the lamp next to Dametrix's left shoulder.

Now the light started flickering on and off, showing glowing red eyes in the dark. A dozen cops came from outside and ran into the house and reached the stairs. Shots were fired. Some of the cops fell down the stairs, unable to breathe, and two policemen stayed behind to help the ones that fell. Others ran towards Dametrix and jumped on him. Some couldn't get close to him.

Dametrix fell and saw, under the bed, the red eyes and a sinister smile.

"Stop resisting arrest you little punk," one of the cops said. They walked him to the patrol car. The neighborhood was lit up with the red-blue lights from all the patrol cars. All the neighbors were outside their houses in their pajamas watching him.

Derica, her hair in a messy ponytail, hid in the bushes and watched.

Sirens wailed as he sat in the back of the car. The cop on the driver's side looked back at him in the rearview mirror and said, "How did you do that kid?"

The other cop in the passenger seat said, "Aren't you that kid I hear about in Queens High? My son talks about you, says you can do some magic trick. Is that what you are, a magician? Did you release some gas in your house?

Is that why we couldn't breathe or walk?"

Dametrix didn't answer.

At the station, he sat in the middle of a concrete room. Handcuffed to the table. Dark mirrored walls surrounded him. There was a metal door to his left. A camera on the ceiling pointed at him.

"Hello," said a Caucasian man in a brown suit who appeared at least six feet tall. "I believe your name is Dutch Dametrix. I'm Detective Wayne Doyle. I'm sorry to hear about your grandma. Do you want to tell me what happened? This isn't the time to be silent, this is your chance to get your story out and have someone listen to you."

Dametrix looked up at him angrily and said, "What's the point? I'm sure you already have your assumptions and see me as guilty."

The detective grabbed a chair and sat at the table across from him. "That's not true. We do have assumptions, but we don't see you as guilty. Just a suspect. That's why I'm here, trying to find out if you are guilty or not."

"If that's true why am I in handcuffs?"

"You're in handcuffs because you were resisting arrest and it took a dozen cops twice your size to handcuff you; three of them you threw halfway across the room. I believe there are   always two sides to a story and that not everything is really what it appears to be. It's the reason why I became a detective. Growing up in these crazy streets I've watched many innocent people go to jail. For things they didn't do or things, they take the blame to protect other people. That's why I'm here listening and need you to tell me the absolute truth. If you lie it will come back and hurt you. Tell me from the beginning what happened."

"I walked into my grandma's room and found her de.. well, the way she was."

"Do you have any ideas what could have happened?"

"No I don't, that's why I need to go find out."

"Are you in a gang? Is there anyone who doesn't like you or your grandma?"

"Gang? Are you serious? You are already judging me. Do I look like I'm in a gang?"

"No one is judging you, I just need to ask all questions to make sure. I have to ask to make sure nothing is left out."

"Besides, I wouldn't know what a gang member looks like. They can look like anything."

"I'm not judging you, just making observations. You do have two tattoos on your shoulder. Six and seven. Seeing how you're underage I'm sure you didn't go get these at the tattoo store."

"My grandma doesn't have enemies that I know about. Everyone loved her. She was the sweet lady that gives you a ride when it's raining outside. Gives homeless people food and a job application 'cause she believes if you're not hurt or in a wheelchair, earning money is better than having someone give it to you. It teaches you morals. So no, I don't think she has enemies. And I'm not in any gangs. These tattoos just happened."

"What do you mean happened? From the sound of your grandma, I'm sure she didn't pay for it. Does she even know about them? Maybe you got mad 'cause she found out."

"Listen I didn't kill my grandma, OK?"

"Tell me why your   room is a mess and there are holes on the walls."

" 'Cause... I slipped and I was looking for sleeping pills so I left it a mess searching."

"Why did you need sleeping pills? It's the weekend, there's no school tomorrow."

"I was just tired of being up – what's the point of that question?"

"What happened to the gun you had in your hand? It says in this report you had one but when they searched the room and you, they couldn't find it."

"It wasn't a gun, it was a toy, and I don't know, maybe it fell outside when they were dragging me."

"You can't be mad at them for being rough with you. If I recall correctly, you were fighting back with them."

"Yeah, take the side of your cops. Just one big gang picking on the little guys and getting away with whatever you want. Hiding behind your badges and fake rules you don't even follow. Seen what you do to people on TV. Let me out of here so I can do some real work and find who's trying to frame me. All you are doing is wasting time."

"Let's get something straight here kid, I'm trying to help you. All I'm doing is trying to save your ass. If I was you, I would watch my tone and how I talk to the person trying to help me. And be grateful. You shouldn't believe everything you hear or see on TV. I could be like you, assuming I am, and release everything I have to the public. And watch your precious TV eat you alive. Yes, there are bad cops.

"When you get older, you will realize that there are bad people everywhere and in every job. Giving the good workers bad names until you walk the streets like we do, putting your life on the line. Then you can talk to me about your same old, recycled speech. There are still good cops trying, regardless of the stuff they get for being cops.

The detective continued, "So far, I don't see why I should help you anymore. You have just been lying to me. I told you to start at the beginning. You started talking to me about the end and withheld information from me."

"What are you talking about? I've been telling you the truth!"

DMT JOURNEYS

"Is that right? So why haven't you told me about Sam, the kid you left in the basement? Don't say it wasn't you because it's the same profile the officers gave − they felt woozy on the scene and spotted a kid who told them, 'It's not a gun it's a toy.'

"You are right about one thing, all we are doing is wasting time," the detective said. "Good luck on your own."

"Fine, you want the truth? I know you're going to think I'm weird and crazy but I'll tell you."

"So how did you make the cops woozy? Was it something you let in the air? Why are your eyes so red? Is it drugs?"

"No. I think I was in another dimension with demons, It happened while I was dreaming. That's how I got the tattoos. The gun came out of my arm and what used to be my sensei taught me how to control my aura so I could better myself and become stronger. I was at the mall with some friends and my friend Sam called and asked to meet him at the haunted house, to find out why the kids were missing from school.

"I got there too late and something killed him. I asked my sensei to teach me to go back in time so I could save him and he said no. I woke up looking for sleeping pills and found my grandma and you know the rest."

Detective Wayne sat in shock with his mouth open. "So you're saying demons are real and they killed your grandma? Is this a joke?" The detective walked towards the door. Dametrix screamed, "You said you wanted the truth, right?"

He got angry and the handcuffs rattled. The detective started to slouch. Breathing heavy, he slowly turned around and looked at Dametrix. "How are you doing that? Kid, stop it, I believe you. Calm down now, stop!" The chains stopped rattling and the detective walked outside.

The other cops told him to stop wasting his time, to throw him at the jury.

Then another officer said, "Did you see the friend's phone call records? See? The friend did call him as he said and video surveillance showed he was at the mall."

The detective walked back into the room with coffee and water in his hands. "You want some water kid? 'Cause I need some coffee after what you told me. I'm stretching out on a limb here, but do you have anyone you can call or go to? I'm going to let you go, but don't skip town or it's automatic jail for you."

With a little smile on his face, Dametrix said, "No, but I'll figure something out. Thank you."

"Sorry kid, I can't let you go out on your own 'cause you're a minor. Wait here for me and I'll see what I can do."

As the detective left the room, Dametrix started yelling and screaming. "What? No! I'm tired of waiting. I've been honest like you asked. Ahhh!"

His aura kept rising and he broke the handcuff chain, walked towards the door, and opened it. One cop looked at the commotion in disbelief, "Hey, what are you doing? Get back in that room!" As the cop rushed in and tried to cuff him, the detective ran up to him. "Don't resist them Dutch. You still can get out of here if you just cooperate." They grabbed Dametrix and put him in a holding cell. The detective looked at him with resigned contempt. "Stop making things difficult for yourself. Just sit here and wait, I'll be back."

"No! My best friend who's a grandma killer is on the loose and you just want me to sit here and wait?!" The detective ignored him and walked away angrily. Dametrix paced back and forth.

Six started to glow. "I can get you out human. I'll shoot the lock and you just step out."

"Won't that make a loud noise? I don't want them looking for me too soon."

"Don't worry about that – either way they're going to look. Just get close and point at the lock and let me at it."

A small fire shot out of Dametrix's left finger at the lock. He raised his aura and ran out, leaving nothing but the sound of wind behind. Detective Wayne turned around. "What is he doing now?" He ran towards the cell only to find it empty. He looked around and grabbed an officer nearby. "Where is he?"

Running towards his home, Dametrix passed the school and stopped in his tracks. Seeing someone leaning towards the Dumpster he pulled out his gun and pointed it. "Get out of the trash now."

Jumping out of the Dumpster was a person with matching black pants and a shirt with messy hair. It was Derica with her hands up. "Don't shoot! Wait, Dametrix, is that you?"

"What are you doing in the trash, Derica?"

"I was searching for clues to help you prove you're innocent. People are saying you killed your grandma. I snuck inside and found a blood-stained pencil that had the school logo on it. I came by the trash and found some more blood on the trash cover and fresh bloody shirts inside like the killer came here to get rid of the evidence. I'm sorry about all this that happened to you. I'm also sorry about earlier at the mall I was interested in your arm.

"It wasn't the only thing I cared about because I had time to think. I realized I care about you to look at what I'm doing, and I really like you. I would like to go on a date with you again when all this blows over. I want you to know that you have someone that will always be by your side."

After a few moments of silence he said, "Thanks, I really do appreciate you helping me and doing all of this."

She smiled and reached to hug him. Dametrix put his hand around her and kissed her. "No, we can't be together. Just go live your life, don't worry about me. I'll be OK."

"What? No, don't go. Everyone in my life has gone away. I always felt like we had a bond. I'm sorry about the mall. I'll do anything to make it up to you and show you."

"It's just not going to work out between us, OK? I have to go."

When he walked away, she fell to her knees and punched the ground until her hands bled.

Dametrix disappeared and ran away, deciding to take a short cut. He spotted two bodies.

"Who is that? Show yourself!"

6   CAUSE AND EFFECT

*T*urning around, he realized it was Stanley and
Martino. A big smile grew on his face. "Man am I happy
to see you guys. I was about to head home to change. I
had a crazy day."

"Yeah, we were out the whole day. Martino and I were

just heading home. We heard you were in jail – and were going to go look for you. How did you get out?"

"What? No, the cops were trying to hold me, asking me annoying questions."

They both asked, "Did the cops ever find out who killed Sam?"

They looked at him. Dametrix replied, "No. I think they're coming after me."

They started to walk into the ally. Dametrix "What's wrong, why did you stop walking? Are you OK Dametrix?" Stanly said.

"How did you guys hear about Sam? The cop told me they haven't released that yet on the news. Plus, you said you were out. You didn't seem too surprised or sad to hear about Sam dying."

Stanley smiled. Martino looked angry.

"Well Martino, damn, he ruined the surprise," Stanly said. "I think the cat is out of the bag. You always were too smart for your own good. We could never keep secrets from him while you hid all of yours. Well, you figured this one out, too. "Both their fingers stretch out like knives.

Stanly disappeared and reappeared behind Dametrix and stabbed Dametrix on the right shoulder.

"What the hell? Really?"

"Yeah really. You deserve it and more."

Dametrix fell to his knees and held his bleeding shoulder. Stanly lifted his left hand and licked the blood that was on it. His fingers had grown long and the nails, longer and sharper. "You talk too much. Yeah, we killed him. We didn't mean to but it had to get done. He was getting too nosy and would mess up the surprise. Plus, we told him to join us, but he refused and turned down power, that fool.

"We suspected he was going to tell you at the haunted house, right? Wasn't that where yah was going to have your secret meeting?"

"Does that mean you killed my grandma too? What the hell did she have to do with this? If you wanted me all you had to do was ask, you cowards. You're supposed to be my best friends."

"Cowards, ha, that's funny. Who left Martino to get choked out by the demon in this very same ally? You were going to go get your glasses, right? That was a lie. We know about that arm of yours and you should have been able to help. You have such power but waste it. Oh, your grandma was an added bonus. We watched her die just like I died in this ally. The demon spoke to me and said he would give me powers better than yours. Explaining all about you to me and Martino."

Dametrix glared at Stanly. "You sold yourselves for stupid powers. Was it worth it? You just became murderers. Is that what you really are Stanly? Well,

Martino? Or is this another thing Stanly dragged you into? You're supposed to be my best friends."

"We didn't do this, it's all your fault. You put him up to this. Remember when I told you I had that dream?"

"Yeah, the demon visited me, but I saw the powers you had, and I went looking for him because I wanted the same thing. So, you're the last one should talk. Do you even know anything about Six? All that time you had it not once did you care to learn. All you did was show off.

Well you're nothing special, just lucky until now. The only special thing about you is how you're going to taste after we kill you."

Dametrix balled up his fist in anger. The ground shook and a crater grew around him. The Dumpsters shook. A great gust of wind began to blow. Martino backed up a little.

"I'm not lucky," Dametrix said. "I make my own luck and I'm starting to feel lucky right about now. What about you, punk?"

He charged towards Stanly, who was laughing. Dametrix disappeared and appeared in front of him, pointing the gun Six in his face, right in front of his mouth. Stanley looked shocked, seeing Dametrix's red eyes with anger in them. Then a shot was fired. Martino looked surprised. Stanly stood with his head bent over, blood dripping out of the side of his face.

The gun had smoke coming out of the barrel. Stanly jumped back. Holding the side of his head where his ear used to be. Dametrix said, "I don't want to hurt you."

Stanly shouted, "Really? Tell that to my other ear because I can't hear you." Martino grabbed onto Dametrix and threw a punch. He landed against the brick wall, which caused the wall to crack.

"What did you do to my friend? Stanly, are you OK?"

"I was once your friend. I told you I wasn't running away," Dametrix said. "I was running to go get my glasses so I could see the demon that was attacking you. My eyes were not as strong as they are now. I told Stanly to help you until I returned, then I realized I couldn't leave you. When I saw Stanly leaving you too, I came back to find him, and you were gone."

Martino kicked Dametrix in the stomach causing him to fall to his knees back on the ground. He continually kicked Dametrix to the ground. Dametrix caught his leg with his right hand and got up. The number seven glowed underneath his shirt. Dametrix took Martino's leg and threw him, then got up and wiped the blood from his nose and mouth.

He pointed the gun Six at Martino, who charged at him, the little Martino that he used to smile and laugh with. Stanly appeared. He hesitated. *I can't do it.* A sharp pain rose from his chest and blood leaked from a new scratch caused by Martino, who ripped off Dametrix's shirt, leaving a big red bloody mark across his chest down to his stomach.

Stanly then kicked him towards the Dumpster which left a big dent. Martino stood while Stanly punched Dametrix and licked the blood off his fingers. Stanly walked towards him and grabbed him, raising him off the ground and holding Dametrix by the neck as he punched him in his stomach. Then he grabbed both his arms from the back, while screaming to Martino.

"Let's go. Don't listen to him," Stanly said to Martino. "Get your revenge. He left you alone by yourself after lying that he would always be there for you. I told you I would make you stronger, so you won't have to ever be scared or weak again. Once we devour his heart, we will have all the power we need."

Martino punched Dametrix in the stomach so hard it caused him to fall to his hands and knees. Then he kicked him in the mouth while Stanly also kicked him on the floor. Dametrix thought, *How do I get out of this one?* Feeling a warmth growing on his right hand he thought, *What's that feeling? I've felt it before.*

Dametrix's right arm started to glow again and he kicked Martino away. Stanly's right arm started to smoke while he held onto Dametrix, whose shoulder was glowing. He let Dametrix go and pushed him away to the floor, falling backwards himself. He quickly got up while smoke came from the right side of his body.

Dametrix was now on the ground coughing and trying to figure out what to do. He felt a warm feeling coming from his right shoulder.

Something came out of Dametrix's right hand that appeared to be a sword that got longer and longer while lifting Dametrix off the ground. Seven on his shoulder was glowing while he held the sword in his right hand and smoke came from his hand. The sword grew hot. The words "Sword of Spirit" appeared on the blade, then disappeared.

Dametrix looked at Stanly with his red eyes and his aura rising again and his right arm glowing and the number six glowing on the left arm.

Stanly screamed, "No that's not fair Where are you getting all this damn power? I will kill you Even if I have to sacrifice someone else."

Dametrix ran with the sword dragging to the ground and sparking as he shot with the gun six. He hit Stanly in the right shoulder then disappeared. Stanly raised his left arm to attack Dametrix and stopped running, watching the hand shoot blood in the air. Stanly did not notice Dametrix behind him and said, "Why don't you lick on that?" Dametrix turned his head to the side and looked at Stanly who was behind him now and furiously raised his left hand with the long sharp fingers. Dametrix yelled,

"Don't do it, you fool."

In a flash Dametrix ducked to dodge the blow and lifted the sword while looking down. That copper iron smell was in the air and he saw blood dripping on the ground. Then something wet slid down his cheeks. That blood he was seeing came from his face and he fell to the ground and felt the weight of Stanly's body on top of him as he had one knee down and one up. He held the burning sword tight in his right hand so it wouldn't tip over to the right or left. Stanly finally got him with a finishing blow. *Is that why I feel a sharp deep pain in my back?* He was crying. Red tears came from his face because he was about to die. Dametrix with his left hand felt under his eyes and his cheek and he looked at the red hand covered in blood.

Stanly stared down at him with tears coming from his eyes and blood running out of his mouth. Dametrix looked lower to see that Stanly was impaled on the sword.

Dametrix got up and Stanly's head fell on his left shoulder. Stanly's eyes opened more as the sword was being removed from the middle of his chest. He whispered in Dametrix's ear, "I hate you for showing off. You deserve to die, not me. All I ever tried to do was be your friend. This is all your fault."

Dametrix pulled out the sword and dropped it. He held onto Stanly and looked toward Martino, who was crying.

"How could you, you bastard! He was our friend." He laid the body next to the sword.

"Really? Even though he said he did all of this on purpose because he hated me."

"No, he didn't really hate you. All he talked about was being like you and wanting to be cool like you and being like Sam and feeling left out. You know his mom is dead. All he ever wanted to do was hang out with you guys because he had no one but you and you deserted him. All of us, we were supposed to be friends to the end, to have each other's back. This is all your fault. Sam, me, and your grandma, I hate you."

Martino ran towards Dametrix with his sharp claws. He ducked and swiped at Dametrix's legs, and punched him in the stomach. Dametrix quickly tried to get up. He disappeared and then reappeared and grabbed Martino's arms. He went behind him and held his arms crossed over his chest. "Stop this Martino, it's not too late. I can still help you, I don't want to lose you too, buddy."

A deep voice uttered, "It's too late for your human."

Martino struggled, then stabbed himself to get to Dametrix. They both then fell alongside Stanly on the ground.

Martino's hand moved towards Stanly's hand.

Dametrix lay on the ground, with Stanly to his far left and watched Martino's eyes water. Martino dragged himself closer to Stanly's left while Dametrix stayed on the right side. Martino grabbed Dametrix's hands as he held Stanly's hands. "I'm sorry we put you through all that. You're still my friend. I don't hate you brother. It was the demon making me do all of this stuff. I could only watch it, I couldn't stop it. Will you forgive me?"

Dametrix tried not to cry and said, "Yeah, of course man. You don't even need to ask, little bro."

"I'm so scared. I don't want to die, Dametrix, help me. Please... I'm too young."

Dametrix struggled and sat up and held onto Martino, trying to wipe the blood from his face and mouth. "Stop trying to move just relax."

Martino looked at him with an innocent child-like look he always had since the first day they met, and remembered the times they played and laughed and the promise that he would be his bro and always look out for him. Martino said, " Do you think God will forgive me?" "Yes, He will. If he doesn't, I'll go get you myself. Because we only have each other." He took one last look at Martino's innocent child-like eyes before he closed them. Passing over his curly hair he said to Martino, "It's all over, now just rest."

Dametrix knelt as little Martino was unable to move, tears pouring out from his eyes. His mouth was full of blood. He held Dametrix's hands tight then slowly let go. Dametrix held Martino's head and stared at his little body, remembering how young he really was. As he gasped for air, he dug graves for them and buried them.

He walked by the road, away from the graves, and a car pulled up behind him. Dametrix felt a heavy feeling of someone following him while a man yelled out to him. "Hey kid, kid, stop! I need to talk to you!"

"Go away and leave me alone, I'm not in the mood to talk."

"Are you sure? I think you'd like to hear what I'm going to tell you plus you look pretty beat up. You need my help. It's an honor that I'm doing this. Not many people get a chance like this."

Dametrix turned and pointed Six in front of the man wearing an expensive, all-black suit and shoes. Standing in front of the black limousine the man did not look worried at all. The limousine that was slowly moving behind the man comes to a complete stop. Then the doors quickly opened. Two guys exited the limousine and pointed guns at Dametrix.

"If you're trying to rob me you just made a big mistake. Leave me alone or I'm killing all of you."

"Hahaha, that's cute kid. Do I look like I need to rob you? Plus, I have more guns than you. Besides if I wanted to hurt you I could have easily done that. You look like you're in no position to fight anyway. Why don't you put down your gun. I can see by the look in your eyes you're ready to die. I like that. Fight till the end.

"Looks like you're having a bit of a bad day huh, kid? Name's Stăna. I've been looking for you ever since you escaped the police department. Don't worry, I paid off all your debt, so consider that as a free gift. Listen, I think you're a special kid. I'd like to help you. I see talent in you, so in return, help me out. Does that make more sense?"

"What the hell do you want from me? You a pervert or something?"

"Ha ha ha sticks and stones kid but no, do I look like a priest to you? Let's go get you cleaned up. If you're going to be around me you can't be looking like that."

"Hey, I never agreed to nothing."

"Where are you going to go? You have nothing left but I won't make you. It's up to you...but time is money so hurry up and pick."

Dametrix stood and held his left shoulder with his arm. The limousine drove away.

Thanks for your purchase!

Check out more dmtjourneys.com

This message is to thank you and to show my appreciation.

D.M.T. Journeys is part one of a book series. Stay tuned for the next installment, to continue on this roller-coaster mystery adventure!